Mack Reynolds

Adaptation & Ultima Thule

OK Publishing 2021

Mack Reynolds
Adaptation & Ultima Thule

The Tale of United Planet

Published by
MUSAICUM
Books

- Advanced Digital Solutions & High-Quality book Formatting -

musaicumbooks@okpublishing.info

2021 OK Publishing

ISBN 978-80-272-7452-9

Contents

Adaptation   11

Forward   13

I.   14

II.   16

III.   20

IV.   26

V.   32

VI.   37

VIL   41

VIII.   43

IX.   47

X.   49

XI.   52

XII.   55

Ultima Thule   59

Adaptation

Forward

Hardly had man solved his basic problems on the planet of his origin than he began to fumble into space. Barely a century had elapsed in the exploration of the Solar System than he began to grope for the stars.

And suddenly, with an all but religious zeal, mankind conceived its fantasy dream of populating the galaxy. Never in the history of the race had fervor reached such a peak and held so long. The question of why was seemingly ignored. Millions of Earth-type planets beckoned and with a lemming-like desperation humanity erupted into them.

But the obstacles were frightening in their magnitude. The planets and satellites of Sol had proven comparatively tractable and those that were suited to man-life were quickly brought under his dominion. But there, of course, he had the advantage of proximity. The time involved in running back and forth to the home planet was meaningless and all Earth's resources could be thrown into each problem's solving.

But a planet a year removed in transportation or even communication? Ay! this was another thing and more than once a million colonists were lost before the Earthlings could adapt to new climates, new flora and fauna, new bacteria-or to factors which the most far out visionary had never fancied, perhaps the lack of something never before missed.

So, mad with the lust to seed the universe with his kind, men sought new methods. To a hundred thousand worlds they sent smaller colonies, as few as a hundred pioneers apiece, and there marooned them, to adapt, if adapt they could.

For a millennium each colony was left to its own resources, to conquer the environment or to perish in the effort.

A thousand years was sufficient. Invariably it was found, on those planets where human life survived at all, man slipped back during his first two or three centuries into a state of barbarism. Then slowly began to inch forward again. There were exceptions and the progress on one planet never exactly duplicated that on another, however the average was surprisingly close to both nadir and zenith, in terms of evolution of society.

In a thousand years it was deemed by the Office of Galactic Colonization such pioneers had largely adjusted to the new environment and were ready for civilization, industrialization and eventual assimilation into the rapidly evolving Galactic Commonwealth.

Of course, even from the beginning, new and unforeseen problems manifested themselves...

from "Man In Antiquity"

published in Terra City, Sol
Galactic Year 3,502.

I.

the Co-ordinator said, "I suppose I'm an incurable romantic. You see, I hate to see you go." Academician Amschel Mayer was a man in early middle years; Dr. Leonid Plekhanov, his contemporary. They offset one another; Mayer thin and high-pitched, his colleague heavy, slow and dour. Now they both showed their puzzlement.

The Co-ordinator added, "Without me."

Plekhanov kept his massive face blank. It wasn't for him to be impatient with his superior. Nevertheless, the ship was waiting, stocked and crewed.

Amschel Mayer said, "Certainly a last minute chat can't harm." Inwardly he realized the other man's position. Here was a dream coming true, and Mayer and his fellows were the last thread that held the Co-ordinator's control over the dream. When they left, half a century would pass before he could again check developments.

The Co-ordinator became more businesslike. "Yes," he said, "but I have more in mind than a chat. Very briefly, I wish to go over your assignment. Undoubtedly redundant, but if there are questions, no matter how seemingly trivial, this is the last opportunity to air them."

What possible questions could there be at this late date? Plekhanov thought.

The department head swiveled slowly in his chair and then back again as he talked. "You are the first-the first of many, many such teams. The manner in which you handle your task will effect man's eternity. Obviously, since upon your experience we will base our future policies on interstellar colonization." His voice lost volume. "The position in which you find yourselves should be humbling."

"It is," Amschel Mayer agreed. Plekhanov nodded his head.

The Co-ordinator nodded, too. "However, the situation is as near ideal as we could hope. Rigel's planets are all but unbelievably Earthlike. Almost all our flora and fauna have been adaptable. Certainly our race has been."

"These two are the first of the seeded planets. Almost a thousand years ago we deposited small bodies of colonists upon each of them. Since then we have periodically checked, from a distance, but never intruded." His eyes went from one of his listeners to the other. "No comments or questions, thus far?"

Mayer said, "This is one thing that surprises me. The colonies are so small to begin with. How could they possibly populate a whole world in one millennium?"

The Co-ordinator said, "Man adapts, Amschel. Have you studied the development of the United States? During her first century and a half the need was for population to fill the vast lands wrested from the Amer-Inds. Families of eight, ten, and twelve children were the common thing, much larger ones were not unknown. And the generations crowded one against another; a girl worried about spinsterhood if she reached seventeen unwed. But in the next century? The frontier vanished, the driving need for population was gone. Not only were drastic immigration laws passed, but the family shrunk rapidly until by mid-Twentieth Century the usual consisted of two or three children, and even the childless family became increasingly common."

Mayer frowned impatiently, "But still, a thousand years. There is always famine, war, disease ..."

Plekhanov snorted patronizingly. "Forty to fifty generations, Amschel? Starting with a hundred colonists? Where are your mathematics?"

The Co-ordinator said, "The proof is there. We estimate that each of Rigel's planets now supports a population of nearly one billion."

"To be more exact," Plekhanov rumbled, "some nine hundred million on Genoa, seven and a half on Texcoco."

Mayer smiled wryly. "I wonder what the residents of each of these planets call their worlds. Hardly the same names we have arbitrarily bestowed."

14

'Probably each call theirs *The World*," the Co-ordinator smiled. "After all, the basic language, in spite of a thousand years, is still Amer-English. However, I assume you are familiar with our method of naming. The most advanced culture on Rigel's first planet is to be compared to the Italian cities during Europe's feudalistic era. We have named that planet Genoa. The most advanced nation of the second planet is comparable to the Aztecs at the time of the conquest. We considered Tenochtitlán but it seemed a tongue twister, so Texcoco is the alternative."

'Modernizing Genoa," Mayer mused, "should be considerably easier than the task on semiprimitive Texcoco."

Plekhanov shrugged, "Not necessarily."

The Co-ordinator held up a hand and smiled at them. "Please, no debates on methods at present. An hour from now you will be in space with a year of travel before you. During that time you'll have opportunity for discussion, debate and hair pulling on every phase of your problem."

His expression became more serious. "You are acquainted with the unique position you assume. These colonists are in your control to an extent no small group has ever dominated millions of others before. No Caesar ever exerted the power that will be in your educated hands. For a half century you will be as gods. Your science, your productive know-how, your medicine-if it comes to that, your weapons-are many centuries in advance of theirs. As I said before, your position should be humbling."

Mayer squirmed in his chair. "Why not check upon us, say, once every decade? In all, our ship's company numbers but sixteen persons. Almost anything could happen. If you were to send a department craft each ten years..."

The Co-ordinator was shaking his head. "Your qualifications are as high as anyone available. Once on the scene you will begin accumulating information which we, here in Terra City, do not have. Were we to send another group in ten years to check upon you, all they could do would be interfere in a situation all the factors with which they would not be cognizant."

Amschel Mayer shifted nervously. "But no matter how highly trained, nor how earnest our efforts, we still may fail." His voice worried. "The department cannot expect guaranteed success. After all, we are the first."

'Admittedly. Your group is first to approach the hundreds of thousands of planets we have seeded. If you fail, we will use your failure to perfect the eventual system we must devise for future teams. Even your failure would be of infinite use to us." He lifted and dropped a shoulder. "I have no desire to undermine your belief in yourselves but-how are we to know? —perhaps there will be a score of failures before we find the ideal method of quickly bringing these primitive colonies into our Galactic Commonwealth."

The Co-ordinator came to his feet and sighed. He still hated to see them go. "If there is no other discussion..."

II

Specialist Joseph Chessman stood stolidly before a viewing screen. Theoretically he was on watch. Actually his eyes were unseeing, there was nothing to see. The star pattern changed so slowly as to be all but permanent.

Not that every other task on board was not similar. One man could have taken the *Pedagogue* from the Solar System to Rigel, just as easily as its sixteen-hand crew was doing. Automation at its ultimate, not even the steward department had tasks adequately to fill the hours.

He had got beyond the point of yawning, his mind was a blank during these hours of duty. He was a stolid, bear of a man, short and massive of build.

A voice behind him said, "Second watch reporting. Request permission to take over the bridge."

Chessman turned and it took a brief moment for the blankness in his eyes to fade into life. "Hello Kennedy, you on already? Seems like I just got here." He muttered in self-contradiction, "Or that I've been here a month."

Technician Jerome Kennedy grinned. "Of course, if you want to stay..."

Chessman said glumly, "What difference does it make where you are? What are they doing in the lounge?"

Kennedy looked at the screen, not expecting to see anything and accomplishing just that. "Still on their marathon argument."

Joe Chessman grunted.

Just to be saying something, Kennedy said, "How do you stand in the big debate?"

"I don't know. I suppose I favor Plekhanov. How we're going to take a bunch of savages and teach them modern agriculture and industrial methods in fifty years under democratic institutions, I don't know. I can see them putting it to a vote when we suggest fertilizer might be a good idea." He didn't feel like continuing the conversation. "See you later, Kennedy," and then, as an afterthought, formally, "Relinquishing the watch to Third Officer."

As he left the compartment, Jerry Kennedy called after him, "Hey, what's the course!"

Chessman growled over his shoulder, "The same it was last month, and the same it'll be next month." It wasn't much of a joke but it was the only one they had between themselves.

In the ship's combination lounge and mess he drew a cup of coffee. Joe Chessman, among whose specialties were propaganda and primitive politics, was third in line in the expedition's hierarchy. As such he participated in the endless controversy dealing with overall strategy but only as a junior member of the firm. Amschel Mayer and Leonid Plekhanov were the center of the fracas and right now were at it hot and heavy.

Joe Chessman listened with only half interest. He settled into a chair on the opposite side of the lounge and sipped at his coffee. They were going over their old battlefields, assaulting ramparts they'd stormed a thousand times over.

Plekhanov was saying doggedly, "Any planned economy is more efficient than any unplanned one. What could be more elementary than that? How could anyone in his right mind deny that?"

And Mayer snapped, "I deny it. That term *planned economy* covers a multitude of sins. My dear Leonid, don't be an idiot..."

"I beg your pardon, sir!"

"Oh, don't get into one of your huffs, Plekhanov."

They were at that stage again.

* * * * *

Technician Natt Roberts entered, a book in hand, and sent the trend of conversation in a new direction. He said, worriedly, "I've been studying up on this and what we're confronted with is two different ethnic periods, barbarism and feudalism. Handling them both at once doubles our problems."

One of the junior specialists who'd been sitting to one side said, "I've been thinking about that and I believe I've got an answer. Why not all of us concentrate on Texcoco? When we've brought them to the Genoa level, which shouldn't take more than a decade or two, then we can start working on the Genoese, too."

Mayer snapped, "And by that time we'll have hardly more than half our fifty years left to raise the two of them to an industrial technology. Don't be an idiot, Stevens."

Stevens flushed his resentment.

Plekhanov said slowly, "Besides, I'm not sure that, given the correct method, we cannot raise Texcoco to an industrialized society in approximately the same time it will take to bring Genoa there."

Mayer bleated a sarcastic laugh at that opinion.

Natt Roberts tossed his book to the table and sank into a chair. "If only one of them had maintained itself at a reasonable level of development, we'd have had help in working with the other. As it is, there are only sixteen of us." He shook his head. "Why did the knowledge held by the original colonists melt away? How can an intelligent people lose such basics as the smelting of iron, gunpowder, the use of coal as a fuel?"

Plekhanov was heavy with condescension. "Roberts, you seem to have entered upon this expedition with a lack of background. Consider. You put down a hundred colonists, products of the most advanced culture. Among these you have one or two who can possibly repair an I.B.M. machine, but is there one who can smelt iron, or even locate the ore? We have others who could design an automated textile factory, but do any know how to weave a blanket on a hand loom?

"The first generation gets along well with the weapons and equipment brought with them from Earth. They maintain the old ways. The second generation follows along but already ammunition for the weapons runs short, the machinery imported from Earth needs parts. There is no local economy that can provide such things. The third generation begins to think of Earth as a legend and the methods necessary to survive on the new planet conflict with those the first settlers imported. By the fourth generation, Earth is no longer a legend but a fable..."

"But the books, the tapes, the films ..." Roberts injected.

"Go with the guns, the vehicles and the other things brought from Earth. On a new planet there is no leisure class among the colonists. Each works hard if the group is to survive. There is no time to write new books, nor to copy the old, and the second and especially the third generation are impatient of the time needed to learn to read, time that should be spent in the fields or at the chase. The youth of an industrial culture can spend twenty years and more achieving a basic education before assuming adult responsibilities but no pioneer society can afford to allow its offspring to so waste its time."

Natt Roberts was being stubborn. "But still, a few would carry the torch of knowledge."

Plekhanov nodded ponderously. "For a while. But then comes the reaction against these nonconformists, these crackpots who, by spending time at books, fail to carry their share of the load. One day they wake up to find themselves expelled from the group-if not knocked over the head."

* * * * *

Joe Chessman had been following Plekhanov's argument. He said dourly, "But finally the group conquers its environment to the point where a minimum of leisure is available again. Not for everybody, of course."

Amschel Mayer bounced back into the discussion. "Enter the priest, enter the war lord. Enter the smart operator who talks or fights himself into a position where he's free from drudgery."

Joe Chessman said reasonably, "If you don't have the man with leisure, society stagnates. Somebody has to have time off for thinking, if the whole group is to advance."

"Admittedly!" Mayer agreed. "I'd be the last to contend that an upper class is necessarily parasitic."

Plekhanov grumbled, "We're getting away from the subject. In spite of Mayer's poorly founded opinions, it is quite obvious that only a collectivized economy is going to enable these Rigel planets to achieve an industrial culture in as short a period as half a century."

Amschel Mayer reacted as might have been predicted. "Look here, Plekhanov, we have our own history to go by. Man made his greatest strides under a freely competitive system."

"Well now ..." Chessman began.

"Prove that!" Plekhanov insisted loudly. "Your so-called free economy countries such as England, France and the United States began their industrial revolution in the early part of the nineteenth century. It took them a hundred years to accomplish what the Soviets did in fifty, in the next century."

"Just a *moment*, now," Mayer simmered. "That's fine, but the Soviets were able to profit by the pioneering the free countries did. The scientific developments, the industrial techniques, were handed to her on a platter."

Specialist Martin Gunther, thus far silent, put in his calm opinion. "Actually, it seems to me the fastest industrialization comes under a paternal guidance from a more advanced culture. Take Japan. In 1854 she was opened to trade by Commodore Perry. In 1871 she abolished feudalism and encouraged by her own government and utilizing the most advanced techniques of a sympathetic West, she began to industrialize." Gunther smiled wryly, "Soon to the dismay of the very countries that originally sponsored bringing her into the modern world. By 1894 she was able to wage a successful war against China and by 1904 she took on and trounced Czarist Russia. In a period of thirty-five years she had advanced from feudalism to a world power."

Joe Chessman took his turn. He said obdurately, "Your paternalistic guidance, given an uncontrolled competitive system, doesn't always work out. Take India after she gained independence from England. She tried to industrialize and had the support of the free nations. But what happened?"

Plekhanov leaned forward to take the ball. "Yes! There's your classic example. Compare India and China. China had a planned industrial development. None of this free competition nonsense. In ten years time they had startled the world with their advances. In twenty years —"

"Yes," Stevens said softly, "but at what price?"

Plekhanov turned on him. "At any price!" he roared. "In one generation they left behind the China of famine, flood, illiteracy, war lords and all the misery that had been China's throughout history."

Stevens said mildly, "Whether in their admitted advances they left behind all the misery that had been China's is debatable, sir."

Plekhanov began to bellow an angry retort but Amschel Mayer popped suddenly to his feet and lifted a hand to quiet the others. "Our solution has just come to me!"

Plekhanov glowered at him.

Mayer said excitedly, "Remember what the Co-ordinator told us? This expedition of ours is the first of its type. Even though we fail, the very mistakes we make will be invaluable. Our task is to learn how to bring backward peoples into an industrialized culture in roughly half a century."

The messroom's occupants scowled at him. Thus far he'd said nothing new.

Mayer went on enthusiastically. "Thus far in our debates we've had two basic suggestions on procedure. I have advocated a system of free competition; my learned colleague has been of the opinion that a strong state and a planned, not to say totalitarian, economy would be the quicker." He paused dramatically. "Very well, I am in favor of trying them both."

They regarded him blankly.

He said with impatience, "There are two planets, at different ethnic periods it is true, but not so far apart as all that. Fine, eight of us will take Genoa and eight Texcoco."

Plekhanov rumbled, "Fine, indeed. But which group will have the use of the *Pedagogue* with its library, its laboratories, its shops, its weapons?"

For a moment, Mayer was stopped but Joe Chessman growled, "That's no problem. Leave her in orbit around Rigel. We've got two small boats with which to ferry back and forth. Each group could have the use of her facilities any time they wished."

"I suppose we could have periodic conferences," Plekhanov said. "Say once every decade to compare notes and make further plans, if necessary."

Natt Roberts was worried. "We had no such instructions from the Co-ordinator. Dividing our forces like that."

Mayer cut him short. "My dear Roberts, we were given *carte blanche*. It is up to us to decide procedure. Actually, this system realizes twice the information such expeditions as ours might ordinarily offer."

"Texcoco for me," Plekhanov grumbled, accepting the plan in its whole. "The more backward of the two, but under my guidance in half a century it will be the more advanced, mark me."

"Look here," Martin Gunther said. "Do we have two of each of the basic specialists, so that we can divide the party in such a way that neither planet will miss out in any one field?"

Amschel Mayer was beaming at the reception of his scheme. "The point is well taken, my dear Martin, however you'll recall that our training was deliberately made such that each man spreads over several fields. This in case, during our half century without contact, one or more of us meets with accident. Besides, the *Pedagogue's* library is such that any literate can soon become effective in any field to the extent needed on the Rigel planets."

III.

Joe Chessman was at the controls of the space lighter. At his side sat Leonid Plekhanov and behind them the other six members of their team. They had circled Texcoco twice at great altitude, four times at a lesser one. Now they were low enough to spot man-made works.

"Nomadic," Plekhanov muttered. "Nomadic and village cultures."

"A few dozen urbanized cultures," Chessman said. "Whoever compared the most advanced nation to the Aztecs was accurate, except for the fact that they base themselves along a river rather than on a mountain plateau."

Plekhanov said, "Similarities to the Egyptians and Sumerians." He looked over his beefy shoulder at the technician who was photographing the areas over which they passed. "How does our geographer progress, Roberts?"

Natt Roberts brought his eyes up from his camera viewer. "I've got most of what we'll need for a while, sir."

Plekhanov turned back to Chessman. "We might as well head for their principal city, the one with the pyramids. We'll make initial contact there. I like the suggestion of surplus labor available."

20

"Surplus labor?" Chessman said, setting the controls. "How do you know?"

"Pyramids," Plekhanov rumbled. "I've always been of the opinion that such projects as pyramids, whether they be in Yucatan or Egypt, are make-work affairs. A priesthood, or other ruling clique, keeping its people busy and hence out of mischief."

Chessman adjusted a speed lever and settled back. "I can see their point."

"But I don't agree with it," Plekhanov said ponderously. "A society that builds pyramids is a static one. For that matter any society that resorts to make-work projects to busy its citizenry has something basically wrong."

Joe Chessman said sourly, "I wasn't supporting the idea, just understanding the view of the priesthoods. They'd made a nice thing for themselves and didn't want to see anything happen to it. It's not the only time a group in the saddle has held up progress for the sake of remaining there. Priests, slave-owners, feudalistic barons, or bureaucrats of a twentieth-century police state, a ruling clique will never give up power without pressure."

Barry Watson leaned forward and pointed down and to the right. "There's the river," he said. "And there's their capital city."

The small spacecraft settled at decreasing speed.

Chessman said, "The central square? It seems to be their market, by the number of people."

'I suppose so," Plekhanov grunted. "Right there before the largest pyramid. We'll remain inside the craft for the rest of today and tonight."

Natt Roberts, who had put away his camera, said, "But why? It's crowded in here."

'Because I said so," Plekhanov rumbled. "This first impression is important. Our flying machine is undoubtedly the first they've seen. We've got to give them time to assimilate the idea and then get together a welcoming committee. We'll want the top men, right from the beginning."

"The equivalent of the Emperor Montezuma meeting Cortez, eh?" Barry Watson said. "A real red carpet welcome."

The *Pedagogue's* space lighter settled to the plaza gently, some fifty yards from the ornately decorated pyramid which stretched up several hundred feet and was topped by a small temple-like building.

Chessman stretched and stood up from the controls. "Your anthropology ought to be better than that, Barry," he said. "There was no Emperor Montezuma and no Aztec Empire, except in the minds of the Spanish." He peered out one of the heavy ports. "And by the looks of this town we'll find an almost duplicate of Aztec society. I don't believe they've even got the wheel."

The eight of them clustered about the craft's portholes, taking in the primitive city that surrounded them. The square had emptied at their approach, and now the several thousand citizens that had filled it were peering fearfully from street entrances and alleyways.

Cogswell, a fiery little technician, said, "Look at them! It'll take hours before they drum up enough courage to come any closer. You were right, doctor. If we left the boat now, we'd make fools of ourselves trying to coax them near enough to talk."

Watson said to Joe Chessman "What do you mean, no Emperor Montezuma?"

Chessman said absently, as he watched, "When the Spanish got to Mexico they didn't understand what they saw, being musclemen rather than scholars. And before competent witnesses came on the scene, Aztec society was destroyed. The conquistadors, who did attempt to describe Tenochtitlán, misinterpreted it. They were from a feudalistic world and tried to portray the Aztecs in such terms. For instance, the large Indian community houses they thought were palaces. Actually, Montezuma was a democratically elected war chief of a confederation of three tribes which militarily dominated most of the Mexican valley. There was no empire because Indian society, being based on the clan, had no method of assimilating newcomers. The Aztec armies could loot and they could capture prisoners for their sacrifices, but they had no system of bringing their conquered enemies into the nation. They hadn't reached that far in the evolution of society. The Incas could have taught them a few lessons."

Plekhanov nodded. "Besides, the Spanish were fabulous liars. In Cortez's attempt to impress Spain's king, he built himself up far beyond reality. To read his reports you'd think the pueblo of Mexico had a population pushing a million. Actually, if it had thirty thousand it was doing well. Without a field agriculture and with their primitive transport, they must have been hard put to feed even that large a town."

A tall, militarily erect native strode from one of the streets that debouched into the plaza and approached to within twenty feet of the space boat. He stared at it for at least ten full minutes then spun on his heel and strode off again in the direction of one of the stolidly built stone buildings that lined the square on each side except that which the pyramid dominated.

Cogswell chirped, "Now that he's broken the ice, in a couple of hours kids will be scratching their names on our hull."

* * * * *

In the morning, two or three hours after dawn, they made their preparations to disembark. Of them all, only Leonid Plekhanov was unarmed. Joe Chessman had a heavy handgun holstered at his waist. The rest of the men carried submachine guns. More destructive weapons were hardly called for, nor available for that matter; once world government had been established on Earth the age-old race for improved arms had fallen away.

Chessman assumed command of the men, growled brief instructions. "If there's any difficulty, remember we're civilizing a planet of nearly a billion population. The life or death of a few individuals is meaningless. Look at our position scientifically, dispassionately. If it becomes necessary to use force-we have the right and the might to back it up. MacBride, you stay with the ship. Keep the hatch closed and station yourself at the fifty-caliber gun."

The natives seemed to know intuitively that the occupants of the craft from the sky would present themselves at this time. Several thousands of them crowded the plaza. Warriors, armed with spears and bronze headed war clubs, kept the more adventurous from crowding too near.

The hatch opened, the steel landing stair snaked out, and the hefty Plekhanov stepped down, closely followed by Chessman. The others brought up the rear, Watson, Roberts, Stevens, Hawkins and Cogswell. They had hardly formed a compact group at the foot of the spacecraft than the ranks of the natives parted and what was obviously a delegation of officials approached them. In the fore was a giant of a man in his late middle years, and at his side a cold-visaged duplicate of him, obviously a son.

Behind these were variously dressed others, military, priesthood, local officials, by their appearance.

Ten feet from the newcomers they stopped. The leader said in quite understandable Amer-English, "I am Taller, Khan of all the People. Our legends tell of you. You must be from First Earth." He added with a simple dignity, a quiet gesture, "Welcome to the World. How may we serve you?"

Plekhanov said flatly, "The name of this planet is Texcoco and the inhabitants shall henceforth be called Texcocans. You are correct, we have come from Earth. Our instructions are to civilize you, to bring you the benefits of the latest technology, to prepare you to enter the community of planets." Phlegmatically he let his eyes go to the pyramids, to the temples, the large community dwelling quarters. "We'll call this city Tula and its citizens Tulans."

Taller looked thoughtfully at him, not having missed the tone of arrogant command. One of the group behind the Khan, clad in gray flowing robes, said to Plekhanov, mild reproof in his voice, "My son, we are the most advanced people on ... Texcoco. We have thought of ourselves as civilized. However, we —"

Plekhanov rumbled, "I am not your son, old man, and you are far short of civilization. We can't stand here forever. Take us to a building where we can talk without these crowds staring at us. There is much to be done."

Taller said, "This is Mynor, Chief Priest of the People."

The priest bowed his head, then said, "The People are used to ceremony on outstanding occasions. We have arranged for suitable sacrifices to the gods. At their completion, we will proclaim a festival. And then —"

The warriors had cleared a way through the multitude to the pyramid and now the Earthlings could see a score of chained men and women, nude save for loin cloths and obviously captives.

Plekhanov made his way toward them, Joe Chessman at his right and a pace to the rear. The prisoners stood straight and, considering their position, with calm.

Plekhanov glared at Taller. "You were going to kill these?"

The Khan said reasonably, "They are not of the People. They are prisoners taken in battle."

Mynor said, "Their lives please the gods."

"There are no gods, as you probably know," Plekhanov said flatly. "You will no longer sacrifice prisoners."

A hush fell on the Texcocans. Joe Chessman let his hand drop to his weapon. The movement was not lost on Taller's son, whose eyes narrowed.

The Khan looked at the burly Plekhanov for a long moment. He said slowly, "Our institutions fit our needs. What would you have us do with these people? They are our enemies. If we turn them loose, they will fight us again. If we keep them imprisoned, they will eat our food. We ... Tulans are not poor, we have food aplenty, for we Tulans, but we cannot feed all the thousands of prisoners we take in our wars."

Joe Chessman said dryly, "As of today there is a new policy. We put them to work."

Plekhanov rumbled at him, "I'll explain our position, Chessman, if you please." Then to the Tulans. "To develop this planet we're going to need the labor of every man, woman and child capable of work."

Taller said, "Perhaps your suggestion that we retire to a less public place is desirable. Will you follow?" He spoke a few words to an officer of the warriors, who shouted orders.

* * * * *

The Khan led the way, Plekhanov and Chessman followed side by side and the other Earthlings, their weapons unostentatiously ready, were immediately behind. Mynor the priest, Taller's son and the other Tulan officials brought up the rear.

In what was evidently the reception hall of Taller's official residence, the newcomers were made as comfortable as fur padded low stools provided. Half a dozen teenaged Tulans brought a cool drink similar to cocoa; it seemed to give a slight lift.

Taller had not become Khan of the most progressive nation on Texcoco by other than his own abilities. He felt his way carefully now. He had no manner of assessing the powers wielded by these strangers from space. He had no intention of precipitating a situation in which he would discover such powers to his sorrow.

He said carefully, "You have indicated that you intend major changes in the lives of the People."

"Of all Texcocans," Plekhanov said, "you Tulans are merely the beginning."

Mynor, the aged priest, leaned forward. "But why? We do not want these changes-whatever they may be. Already the Khan has allowed you to interfere with our worship of our gods. This will mean —"

Plekhanov growled, "Be silent, old man, and don't bother to mention, ever again, your so-called gods. And now, all of you listen. Perhaps some of this will not be new, how much history has come down to you I don't know.

"A thousand years ago a colony of one hundred persons was left here on Texcoco. It will one day be of scholarly interest to trace them down through the centuries but at present the task does not interest us. This expedition has been sent to recontact you, now that you have populated Texcoco and made such adaptations as were necessary to survive here. Our basic task is to modernize your society, to bring it to an industrialized culture."

Plekhanov's eyes went to Taller's son. "I assume you are a soldier?"

Taller said, "This is Reif, my eldest, and by our custom, second in command of the People's armies. As Khan, I am first."

Reif nodded coldly to Plekhanov. "I am a soldier." He hesitated for a moment, then added, "And willing to die to protect the People."

"Indeed," Plekhanov rumbled, "as a soldier you will be interested to know that our first step will involve the amalgamation of all the nations and tribes of this planet. Not a small task. There should be opportunity for you."

Taller said, "Surely you speak in jest. The People have been at war for as long as scribes have records and never have we been stronger than today, never larger. To conquer the world! Surely you jest."

Plekhanov grunted ungraciously. He looked to Barry Watson, a lanky youth, now leaning negligently against the wall, his submachine gun, however, at the easy ready. "Watson, you're our military expert. Have you any opinions as yet?"

"Yes, sir," Watson said easily. "Until we can get iron weapons and firearms into full production, I suggest the Macedonian phalanx for their infantry. They have the horse, but evidently the wheel has gone out of use. We'll introduce the chariot and also heavy carts to speed up logistics. We'll bring in the stirruped saddle, too. I have available for study, works on every cavalry leader from Tamerlane to Jeb Stuart. Yes, sir, I have some ideas."

Plekhanov pursed his heavy lips. "From the beginning we're going to need manpower on a scale never dreamed of locally. We'll adopt a policy of expansion. Those who join us freely will become members of the State with full privileges. Those who resist will be made prisoners of war and used for shock labor on the roads and in the mines. However, a man works better if he has a goal, a dream. Each prisoner will be freed and become a member of the State after ten years of such work."

He turned to his subordinates. "Roberts and Hawkins, you will begin tomorrow to seek the nearest practical sources of iron ore and coal. Wherever you discover them we'll direct our first military expeditions. Chessman and Cogswell, you'll assemble their best artisans and begin their training in such basic advancements as the wheel."

Taller said softly, "You speak of advancement but thus far you have mentioned largely war and on such a scale that I wonder how many of the People will survive. What advancement? We have all we wish."

Plekhanov cut him off with a curt motion of his hand. He indicated the hieroglyphics on the chamber's walls. "How long does it take to learn such writing?"

Mynor, the priest, said, "This is a mystery known only to the priesthood. One spends ten years in preparation to be a scribe."

"We'll teach you a new method which will have every citizen of the State reading and writing within a year."

The Tulans gaped at him.

He moved ponderously over to Roberts, drew from its scabbard the sword bayonet the other had at his hip. He took it and slashed savagely at a stone pillar, gouging a heavy chunk from it. He tossed the weapon to Reif, whose eyes lit up.

"What metals have you been using? Copper, bronze? Probably. Well, that's steel. You're going to move into the iron age overnight."

He turned to Taller. "Are your priests also in charge of the health of your people?" he growled. "Are their cures obtained from mumbo-jumbo and a few herbs found in the desert? Within a decade, I'll guarantee you that not one of your major diseases will remain."

He turned to the priest and said, "Or perhaps this will be the clincher for some of you. How many years do you have, *old man*?"

Mynor said with dignity, "I am sixty-four."

Plekhanov said churlishly, "And I am two hundred and thirty-three." He called to Stevens, "I think you're our youngest. How old are you?"

Stevens grinned, "Hundred and thirteen, next month."

Mynor opened his mouth, closed it again. No man but would prolong his youth. Of a sudden he felt old, old.

Plekhanov turned back to Taller. "Most of the progress we have to offer is beyond your capacity to understand. We'll give you freedom from want. Health. We'll give you advances in every art. We'll eventually free every citizen from drudgery, educate him, give him the opportunity to enjoy intellectual curiosity. We'll open the stars to him. All these things the coming of the State will eventually mean to you."

Tula's Khan was not impressed. "This you tell us, man from First Earth. But to achieve these you plan to change every phase of our lives and we are happy with ... Tula ... the way it is. I say this to you. There are but eight of you and many, many of us. We do not want your ... State. Return from whence you came."

Plekhanov shook his massive head at the other. "Whether or not *you* want these changes they will be made. If you fail to co-operate, we will find someone who will. I suggest you make the most of it."

Taller arose from the squat stool upon which he'd been seated. "I have listened and I do not like what you have said. I am Khan of all the People. Now leave in peace, or I shall order my warriors ..."

"Joe," Plekhanov said flatly. "Watson!"

Joe Chessman took his heavy gun from its holster and triggered it twice. The roar of the explosions reverberated thunderously in the confined space, deafening all, and terrifying the Tulans. Bright red colored the robes the Khan wore, colored them without beauty. Bright red splattered the floor.

Leonid Plekhanov stared at his second in command, wet his thick lips. "Joe," he sputtered. "I hadn't ... I didn't expect you to be so ... hasty."

Joe Chessman growled, "We've got to let them know where we stand, right now, or they'll never hold still for us. Cover the doors, Watson, Roberts." He motioned to the others with his head. "Cogswell, Hawkins, Stevens, get to those windows and watch."

Taller was a crumbled heap on the floor. The other Texcocans stared at his body in shocked horror.

All expect Reif.

Reif bent down over his father's body for a moment, and then looked up, his lips white, at Plekhanov. "He is dead."

Leonid Plekhanov collected himself. "Yes."

Reif's cold face was expressionless. He looked at Joe Chessman who stood stolidly to one side, gun still in hand.

Reif said, "You can supply such weapons to my armies?"

Plekhanov said, "That is our intention, in time."

Reif came erect. "Subject to the approval of the clan leaders, I am now Khan. Tell me more of this State of which you have spoken."

IV.

The sergeant stopped the small company about a quarter of a mile from the city of Bari. His detachment numbered only ten but they were well armed with short swords and blunderbusses and wore mail and steel helmets. On the face of it, they would have been a match for ten times this number of merchants.

It was hardly noon but the sergeant had obviously already been at his wine flask. He leered at them. "And where do you think you go?"

The merchant who led the rest was a thin little man but he was richly robed and astride a heavy black mare. He said, "To Bari, soldier." He drew a paper from a pouch. "I hold this permission from Baron Mannerheim to pass through his lands with my people and chattels."

The leer turned mercenary. "Unfortunately, city man, I can't read. What do you carry on the mules?"

"Personal property, which, I repeat, I have permission to transport over Baron Mannerheim's lands free from harassment from his followers." He added, in irritation, "The baron is a friend of mine, fond of the gifts I give him."

One of the soldiers grunted his skepticism, checked the flint on the lock of his piece, then looked at the sergeant suggestively.

The sergeant said, "As you say, merchant, my lord the baron is fond of gifts. Aren't we all? Unfortunately, I have received no word of your group. My instructions are to stop all intruders upon the baron's lands and, if there is resistance, to slay them and confiscate such properties as they may be carrying."

The merchant sighed and reached into a small pouch. The eyes of the sergeant drooped in greed. The hand emerged with two small coins. "As you say," the merchant muttered bitterly, "we are all fond of gifts. Will you do me the honor to drink my health at the tavern tonight?"

The sergeant said nothing, but his mouth slackened and he fondled the hilt of his sword.

The merchant sighed again and dipped once more into the pouch. This time his hand emerged with half a dozen bits of silver. He handed them down to the other, complaining, "How can a man profit in his affairs if every few miles he must pass another outstretched hand?"

The sergeant growled, "You do not seem to starve, city man. Now, on your way. You are fortunate I am too lazy today to bother going through your things. Besides," and he grinned widely, "the baron gave me personal instructions not to bother you."

The merchant snorted, kicked his heels into his beast's sides and led his half dozen followers toward the city. The soldiers looked after them and howled their amusement. The money was enough to keep them soused for days.

When they were out of earshot, Amschel Mayer grinned his amusement back over his shoulder at Jerome Kennedy. "How'd that come off, Jerry?"

The other sniffed, in mock deprecation. "You're beginning to fit into the local merchant pattern better than the real thing. However, just for the record, I had this, ah, grease gun, trained on them all the time."

Mayer frowned. "Only in extreme emergency, my dear Jerry. The baron would be up in arms if he found a dozen of his men massacred on the outskirts of Bari, and we don't want a showdown at this stage. It's taken nearly a year to build this part we act."

At this time of day the gates of the port city were open and the guards lounged idly. Their captain recognized Amschel Mayer and did no more than nod respectfully.

They wended their way through narrow, cobblestoned streets, avoiding the crowds in the central market area. They pulled up eventually before a house both larger and more ornate than its neighbors. Mayer and Kennedy dismounted from the horses and left their care to the others.

Mayer beat with the heavy knocker on the door and a slot opened for a quick check of his identity. The door opened wide and Technician Martin Gunther let them in.

"The others are here already?" Mayer asked him.

Gunther nodded. "Since breakfast. Baron Leonar, in particular, is impatient."

Mayer said over his shoulder, "All right, Jerry, this is where we put it to them."

They entered the long conference room. A full score of men sat about the heavy wooden table. Most of them were as richly garbed as their host. Most of them in their middle years. All of them alert of eye. All of them confidently at ease.

* * * * *

Amschel Mayer took his place at the table's end and Jerome Kennedy sank into the chair next to him. Mayer took the time to speak to each of his guests individually, then he leaned back and took in the gathering as a whole. He said, "You probably realize that this group consists of the twenty most powerful merchants on the continent."

Olderman nodded. "We have been discussing your purpose in bringing us together, Honorable Mayer. All of us are not friends." He twisted his face in amusement. "In fact, very few of us are friends."

"There is no need for you to be," Mayer said snappishly, "but all are going to realize the need for co-operation. Honorables, I've just come from the city of Ronda. Although I'd paid heavily in advance to the three barons whose lands I crossed. I had to bribe myself through a dozen road-blocks, had to pay exorbitant rates to cross three ferries, and once had to fight off supposed bandits."

One of his guests grumbled, "Who were actually probably soldiers of the local baron who had decided that although you had paid him transit fee, it still might be profitable to go through your goods."

Mayer nodded. "Exactly, my dear Honorable, and that is why we've gathered."

Olderman had evidently assumed spokesmanship for the others. Now he said warily, "I don't understand."

"Genoa, if you'll pardon the use of this name to signify the planet upon which we reside, will never advance until trade has been freed from these bandits who call themselves lords and barons."

Eyebrows reached for hairlines.

Olderman's eyes darted about the room, went to the doors. "Please," he said, "the servants."

"My servants are safe," Mayer said.

One of his guests was smiling without humor. "You seem to forget, Honorable Mayer, that I carry the title of baron."

Mayer shook his head. "No, Baron Leonar. But neither do you disagree with what I say. The businessman, the merchant, the manufacturer on Genoa today, is only tolerated. Were it not for the fact that the barons have no desire to eliminate such a profitable source of income, they would milk us dry overnight."

Someone shrugged. "That is the way of things. We are lucky to have wrested, bribed and begged as many favors from the lords as we have. Our twenty cities all have charters that protect us from complete despoilation."

Mayer twisted excitedly in his chair. "As of today, things begin to change. Jerry, that platen press."

Jerry Kennedy left the room momentarily and returned with Martin Gunther and two of the servants. While the assembled merchants looked on, in puzzled silence, Mayer's assistants set up the press and a stand holding two fonts of fourteen-point type. Jerry took up a printer's stick and gave running instructions as he demonstrated. Gunther handed around pieces of the type until all had examined it, while his colleague set up several lines. Kennedy transposed the lines to a chase, locked it up and placed the form to one side while he demonstrated inking the small press, which was operated by a foot pedal. He mounted the form in the press, took a score of sheets of paper and rapidly fed them, one by one. When they were all printed, he stopped pumping and Gunther handed the still wet finished product around to the audience.

Olderman stared down at the printed lines, scowled in concentration, wet his lips in sudden comprehension.

But it was merchant Russ who blurted, "This will revolutionize the inscribing of books. Why, it can well take it out of the hands of the Temple! With such a machine I could make a hundred books —"

Mayer was beaming. "Not a hundred, Honorable, but a hundred thousand!"

The others stared at him as though he was demented. "A hundred thousand," one said. "There are not that many literate persons on the continent."

"There will be," Mayer crowed. "This is but one of our levers to pry power from the barons. And here is another." He turned to Russ. "Honorable Russ, your city is noted for the fine quality of its steel, of the swords and armor you produce."

Russ nodded. He was a small man fantastically rich in his attire. "This is true, Honorable Mayer."

Mayer said, tossing a small booklet to the other, "I have here the plans for a new method of making steel from pig iron. The Bessemer method, we'll call it. The principle involved is the oxidation of the impurities in the iron by blowing air through the molten metal."

Amschel Mayer turned to still another. "And your town is particularly noted for its fine textiles." He looked to his assistants. "Jerry, you and Gunther bring in those models of the power loom and the spinning jenny."

While they were gone, he said, "My intention is to assist you to speed up production. With this in mind, you'll appreciate the automatic flying shuttle that we'll now demonstrate."

Kennedy and Gunther re-entered accompanied by four servants and a mass of equipment. Kennedy muttered to Amschel Mayer, "I feel like the instructor of a handicrafts class."

Half an hour later, Kennedy and Gunther wound up passing out pamphlets to the awed merchant guests. Kennedy said, "This booklet will give details on construction of the equipment and its operation."

Mayer pursed his lips. "Your people will be able to assimilate only so fast, so we won't push them. Later, you'll be interested in introducing the mule spinning frame, among other items."

He motioned for the servants to remove the printing press and textile machinery. "We now come to probably the most important of the devices I have to introduce to you today. Because of size and weight, I've had constructed only a model. Jerry!"

Jerry Kennedy brought to the heavy table a small steam engine, clever in its simplicity. He had half a dozen attachments for it. Within moments he had the others around him, as enthusiastic as a group of youngsters with a new toy.

"By the Supreme," Baron Leonar blurted, "do you realize this device could be used instead of waterpower to operate a mill to power the loom demonstrated an hour ago?"

Honorable Russ was rubbing the side of his face thoughtfully. "It might even be adapted to propel a coach. A coach without horses. Unbelievable!"

Mayer chuckled in excitement and clapped his hands. A servant entered with a toy wagon which had been slightly altered. Martin Gunther lifted the small engine, placed it in position atop the wagon, connected it quickly and threw a lever. The wagon moved smoothly forward, the first engine-propelled vehicle of Genoa's industrial revolution.

Martin Gunther smiled widely at Russ. "You mean like this, Honorable?"

Half an hour later they were re-seated, before each of them a small pile of pamphlets, instructions, plans, blueprints.

Mayer said, "I have just one more device to bring to your attention at this time. I wish it were unnecessary but I am afraid otherwise."

He held up for their inspection, a forty-five-caliber bullet. Jerry Kennedy handed around samples to the merchants. They fingered them in puzzlement.

"Honorables," Mayer said, "the barons have the use of gunpowder. Muskets and muzzleloading cannon are available to them both for their wars against each other and their occasional attacks upon our supposedly independent cities. However, this is an advancement on their weapons. This unit includes not only the bullet's lead, but the powder and the cap which will explode it."

They lacked understanding, and showed it.

Mayer said, "Jerry, if you'll demonstrate."

Jerry Kennedy said, "The bullet can be adapted to various weapons, however, this is one of the simplest." He pressed, one after another, a full twenty rounds into the gun's clip.

"Now, if you'll note the silhouette of a man I've drawn on the wooden frame at the end of the room." He pressed the trigger, sent a single shot into the figure.

Olderman nodded. "An improvement in firearms. But —"

Kennedy said, "However, if you are confronted with more than one of the bad guys." He grinned and flicked the gun to full automatic and in a Götterdämmerung of sound in the confines of the room, emptied the clip into his target sending splinters and chips flying and all but demolishing the wooden backdrop.

His audience sat back in stunned horror at the demonstration.

Mayer said now, "The weapon is simple to construct, any competent gunsmith can do it. It is manifest, Honorables, that with your people so equipped your cities will be safe from attack and so will trading caravans and ships."

Russ said shakily, "Your intention is good, Honorable Mayer, however it will be but a matter of time before the barons have solved the secrets of your weapon. Such cannot be held indefinitely. Then we would again be at their mercy."

"Believe me, Honorable," Mayer said dryly, "by that time I will have new weapons to introduce, if necessary. Weapons that make this one a very toy in comparison."

Olderman resumed his office as spokesman. "This demonstration has astounded us, Honorable Mayer, but although we admire your abilities it need hardly be pointed out that it seems unlikely all this could be the product of one brain."

"They are not mine," Mayer admitted. "They are the products of many minds."

"But where —?"

The Earthman shook his head. "I don't believe I will tell you now."

"I see." The Genoese eyed him emotionlessly. "Then the question becomes, *why?*"

Mayer said, "It may be difficult for you to see, but the introduction of each of these will be a nail in feudalism's coffin. Each will increase either production or trade and such increase will lead to the overthrow of feudal society."

Baron Leonar, who had remained largely silent throughout the afternoon, now spoke up. "As you said earlier, although I am a lord myself, my interests are your own. I am a merchant first. However, I am not sure I want the changes these devices will bring. Frankly, Honorable Mayer, I am satisfied with my world as I find it today."

Amschel Mayer smiled wryly at him. "I am afraid you *must* adapt to these new developments."

The baron said coldly, "Why? I do not like to be told I must do something."

"Because, my dear baron, there are three continents on the planet of Genoa. At present there is little trade due to inadequate shipping. But the steam engine I introduce today will soon propel larger craft than you have ever built before."

Russ said, "What has this to do with our being forced to use these devices?"

"Because I have colleagues on the other continents busily introducing them. If you don't adapt, in time competitors will invade your markets, capture your trade, drive you out of business."

Mayer wrapped it up. "Honorables, modernize or go under. It's each man for himself and the devil take the hindmost, if you'll allow a saying from another era."

They remained silent for a long period. Finally Olderman stated bluntly, "The barons are not going to like this."

Jerry Kennedy grinned. "Obviously, that's why we've introduced you to the tommy gun. It's not going to make any difference if they like it or not."

Russ said musingly, "Pressure will be put to prevent the introduction of this equipment."

"We'll meet it," Mayer said, shifting happily in his seat.

Russ added, "The Temple is ever on the side of the barons. The monks will fight against innovations that threaten to disturb the present way."

Mayer said, "Monks usually do. How much property is in the hands of the Temple?"

Russ admitted sourly, "The monks are the greatest landlords of all. I would say at least one third of the land and the serfs belong to the Temple."

"Ah," Mayer said. "We must investigate the possibilities of a Reformation. But that can come later. Now I wish to expand on my reason for gathering you.

"Honorables, Genoa is to change rapidly. To survive, you will have to move fast. I have not introduced these revolutionary changes without self-interest. Each of you are free to use them to his profit, however, I expect a thirty per cent interest."

There was a universal gasp.

Olderman said, "Honorable Mayer, you have already demonstrated your devices. What is there to prevent us from playing you false?"

Mayer laughed. "My dear Olderman, I have other inventions to reveal as rapidly as you develop the technicians, the workers, capable of building and operating them. If you cheat me now, you will be passed by next time."

Russ muttered, "Thirty per cent! Your wealth will be unbelievable."

"As fast as it accumulates, Honorables, it shall be invested. For instance, I have great interest in expanding our inadequate universities. The advances I expect will only be possible if we educate the people. Field serfs are not capable of running even that simple steam engine Jerry demonstrated."

Baron Leonar said, "What you contemplate is mind-shaking. Do I understand that you wish a confederation of all our cities? A joining together to combat the strength of the present lords?"

Mayer was shaking his head. "No, no. As the barons lose power, each of your cities will strengthen and possibly expand to become nations. Perhaps some will unite. But largely you will compete against each other and against the nations of the other continents. In such competition you'll have to show your mettle, or go under. Man develops at his fastest when pushed by such circumstance."

The Earthling looked off, unseeing, into a far corner of the room. "At least, so is my contention. Far away from here a colleague is trying to prove me wrong. We shall see."

V.

Leonid Plekhanov returned to the *Pedagogue* with a certain ceremony. He was accompanied by Joe Chessman, Natt Roberts and Barry Watson of his original group, but four young, hard-eyed, hard-faced and armed Tulans were also in the party. Their space lighter swooped in, nestled to the *Pedagogue's* hull in the original bed it had occupied on the trip from Terra City, and her port opened to the corridors of the mother ship.

Plekhanov, flanked by Chessman and Watson, strode heavily toward the ship's lounge. Natt Roberts and two of the Tulans remained with the small boat. Two of the other natives followed, their eyes darting here, there, in amazement, in spite of their efforts to appear grim and untouched by it all.

Amschel Mayer was already seated at the officer's dining table. His face displayed his irritation at the other's method of presenting himself. "Good Heavens, Plekhanov, what is this, an invasion?"

The other registered surprise.

Mayer indicated the Texcocans. "Do you think it necessary to bring armed men aboard the *Pedagogue*? Frankly, I have not even revealed to a single Genoese the existence of the ship."

Jerry Kennedy was seated to one side, the only member of Mayer's team who had accompanied him for this meeting. Kennedy winked at Watson and Chessman. Watson grinned back but held his peace.

Plekhanov sank into a chair, rumbling, "We hold no secrets from the Texcocans. The sooner they advance to where they can use our libraries and laboratories, the better. And the fact these boys are armed has no significance. My Tulans are currently embarked on a campaign to unite the planet. Arms are sometimes necessary, and Tula, my capital, is somewhat of an armed camp. All able-bodied men —"

Mayer broke in heatedly, "And is this the method you use to bring civilization to Texcoco? Is this what you consider the purpose of the Office of Galactic Colonization? An armed camp! How many persons have you slaughtered thus far?"

"Easy," Joe Chessman growled.

Amschel Mayer spun on him. "I need no instruction from you, Chessman. Please remember I'm senior in charge of this expedition and as such rank you."

Plekhanov thudded a heavy hand on the table. "I'll call my assistants to order, Mayer, if I feel it necessary. Admittedly, when this expedition left Terra City you were the ranking officer. Now, however, we've divided-at your suggestion, please remember. Now there are two independent groups and you no longer have jurisdiction over mine."

"Indeed!" Mayer barked. "And suppose I decide to withhold the use of the *Pedagogue's* libraries and laboratories to you? I tell you, Plekhanov —"

Leonid Plekhanov interrupted him coldly. "I would not suggest you attempt any such step, Mayer."

Mayer glared but suddenly reversed himself. "Let's settle down and become more sensible. This is the first conference of the five we have scheduled. Ten years have elapsed. Actually, of course, we've had some idea of each other's progress since team members occasionally meet on trips back here to the *Pedagogue* to consult the library. I am afraid, my dear Leonid, that your theories on industrialization are rapidly being proven inaccurate."

"Nonsense!"

Mayer said smoothly, "In the decade past, my team's efforts have more than tripled the Genoese industrial potential. Last week one of our steamships crossed the second ocean. We've located petroleum and the first wells are going down. We've introduced a dozen crops that had disappeared through misadventure to the original colonists. And, oh yes, our first railroad is scheduled to begin running between Bari and Ronda next spring. There are six new universities and in the next decade I expect fifty more."

"Very good, indeed," Plekhanov grumbled.

"Only a beginning. The breath of competition, of unharnessed enterprise is sweeping Genoa. Feudalism crumbles. Customs, mores and traditions that have held up progress for a century or more are now on their way out."

Joe Chessman growled, "Some of the boys tell me you've had a few difficulties with this crumbling feudalism thing. In fact, didn't Buchwald barely escape with his life when the barons on your western continent united to suppress all chartered cities?"

Mayer's thin face darkened. "Never fear, my dear Joseph, those barons responsible for shedding the blood of western hemisphere elements of progress will shortly pay for their crimes."

"You've got military problems too, then?" Barry Watson asked.

Mayer's eyes went to him in irritation. "Some of the free cities of Genoa are planning measures to regain their property and rights on the western hemisphere. This has nothing to do with my team, except, of course, in so far as they might sell them supplies or equipment."

The lanky Watson laughed lowly, "You mean like selling them a few quick-firing breech-loaders and trench mortars?"

Plekhanov muttered, "That'll be enough, Barry."

But Mayer's eyes had widened. "How did you know?" He whirled on Plekhanov. "You're spying on my efforts, trying to negate my work!"

Plekhanov rumbled, "Don't be a fool, Mayer. My team has neither the time nor interest to spy on you."

"Then how did you know—"

Barry Watson said mildly, "I was doing some investigation in the ship's library. I ran into evidence that you people had already used the blueprints for breech-loaders and mortars."

Jerry Kennedy came to his feet and rambled over to the messroom's bar. "This seems to be all out spat, rather than a conference to compare progress," he said. "Anybody for a drink? Frankly, that's the next thing I'm going to introduce to Genoa, some halfway decent likker. Do you know what those benighted heathens drink now?"

Watson grinned. "Make mine whisky, Jerry. You've no complaints. Our benighted heathens have a national beverage fermented from a plant similar to cactus. Ought to be drummed out of the human race."

He spoke idly, forgetful of the Tulan guards stationed at the doorway.

* * * * *

Kennedy passed drinks around for everyone save Mayer, who shook his head in distaste. If only for a brief spell, some of the tenseness left the air while the men from Earth sipped their beverages.

Jerry Kennedy said, "Well, you've heard our report. How go things on Texcoco?"

"According to plan," Plekhanov rumbled.

Mayer snorted.

Plekhanov said ungraciously, "Our prime effort is now the uniting of the total population into one strong whole, a super-state capable of accomplishing the goals set us by the Co-ordinator."

Mayer sneered, "Undoubtedly, this goal of yours, this super-state, is being established by force."

"Not always," Joe Chessman said. "Quite a few of the tribes join up on their own. Why not? The State has a lot to offer."

"Such as what?" Kennedy said mildly.

Chessman looked at him in irritation. "Such as advanced medicine, security from famine, military protection from more powerful nations. The opportunity for youth to get an education and find advancement in the State's government-if they've got it on the ball."

"And what happens if they don't *have it on the ball*?"

Chessman growled, "What happens to such under any society? They get the dirty-end-of-the-stick jobs." His eyes went from Kennedy to Mayer. "Are you suggesting you offer anything better?"

Mayer said, "Already on most of Genoa it is a matter of free competition. The person with ability is able to profit from it."

Joe Chessman grunted sour amusement. "Of course, it doesn't help to be the son of a wealthy merchant or a big politician."

Plekhanov took over. "In *any* society the natural leaders come to the top in much the same manner as the big ones come to the top in a bin of potatoes, they just work their way up."

Jerry Kennedy finished his drink and said easily, "At least, those at the top can claim they're the biggest potatoes. Remember back in the twentieth century when Hitler and his gang announced they were the big potatoes in Germany and men of Einstein's stature fled the country-being small potatoes, I suppose."

Amschel Mayer said, "We're getting away from the point. Pray go on, my dear Leonid. You say you are forcibly uniting all Texcoco."

"We are uniting all Texcoco," Plekhanov corrected with a scowl. "Not always by force. And that is by no means our only effort. We are ferreting out the most intelligent of the assimilated peoples and educating them as rapidly as possible. We've introduced iron..."

"And use it chiefly for weapons," Kennedy murmured.

"...Antibiotics and other medicines, a field agriculture, are rapidly building roads..."

"Military roads," Kennedy mused.

"...To all sections of the State, have made a beginning in naval science, and, of course, haven't ignored the arts."

"On the face of it," Mayer nodded, "hardly approaching Genoa."

Plekhanov rumbled indignantly, "We started two ethnic periods behind you. Even the Tulans were still using bronze, but the Genoese had iron and even gunpowder. Our advance is a bit slow to get moving, Mayer, but when it begins to roll —"

Mayer gave his characteristic snort. "A free people need never worry about being passed by a subjected one."

Barry Watson made himself another drink and while doing so looked over his shoulder at Amschel Mayer. "It's interesting the way you throw about that term *free*. Just what type of government do you sponsor?"

Mayer snapped, "Our team does not interfere in governmental forms, Watson. The various nations are free to adapt to whatever local conditions obtain. They range from some under feudalistic domination to countries with varying degrees of republican democracy. Our base of operations in the southern hemisphere is probably the most advanced of all the chartered cities, Barry. It amounts to a city-state somewhat similar to Florence during the Renaissance."

"And your team finds itself in the position of the Medici, I imagine."

"You might use that analogy. The Medici might have been, well, tyrants of Florence, dominating her finances and trade as well as her political government, but they were benevolent tyrants."

"Yeah," Watson grinned. "The thing about a benevolent tyranny, though, is that it's up to the tyrants to decide what's benevolent. I'm not so sure there's a great basic difference between your governing of Genoa and ours of Texcoco."

"Don't be an ass," Mayer snapped. "We are granting the Genoese political freedoms as fast as they can assimilate them."

Joe Chessman growled, "But I imagine it's surprising to find just how slowly they can assimilate. A moment ago you said they were free to form any government they wished. Now you say you feed them what you call freedom, only so fast as they can assimilate it."

"Obviously we encourage them along whatever path we think will most quickly develop their economies," Mayer argued. "That's what we've been sent here to do. We stimulate competition, encourage all progress, political as well as economic."

Plekhanov lumbered to his feet. "Amschel, obviously nothing new has been added to our respective positions by this conference. I propose we adjourn to meet again at the end of the second decade."

Mayer said, "I suppose it would be futile to suggest you give up this impossible totalitarian scheme of yours and reunite the expedition."

Plekhanov merely grunted his disgust.

Jerry Kennedy said, "One thing. What stand have you taken on giving your planet immortality?"

"Immortality?" Watson said. "We haven't it to give."

"You know what I mean. It wouldn't take long to extend the life span double or triple the present."

Amschel Mayer said, "At this stage progress is faster with the generations closer together. A man is pressed when he knows he has only twenty or thirty years of peak efficiency. We on Earth are inclined to settle back and take life as it comes; you younger men are all past the century mark, but none have bothered to get married as yet."

"Plenty of time for that," Watson grinned.

"That's what I mean. But a Texcocan or Genoese feels pressed to wed in his twenties, or earlier, to get his family under way."

"There's another element," Plekhanov muttered. "The more the natives progress the more nearly they'll equal our abilities. I wouldn't want anything to happen to our overall plans. As it is now, their abilities taper off at sixty and they reach senility at seventy or eighty. I think until the end we should keep it this way."

"A cold-blooded view," Kennedy said. "If we extended their life expectancy, their best men would live to be of additional use to planet development."

"But they would not have our dream," Plekhanov rumbled. "Such men might try to subvert us, and, just possibly, might succeed."

"I think Leonid is right," Mayer admitted with reluctance.

* * * * *

Later, in the space lighter heading back for Genoa, Mayer said speculatively, "Did you notice anything about Leonid Plekhanov?"

Kennedy was piloting. "He seems the same irascible old curmudgeon he's always been."

"It seems to me he's become a touch power mad. Could the pressures he's under cause his mind to slip? Obviously, all isn't peaches and cream in that attempt of his to achieve world government on Texcoco."

"Well," Kennedy muttered, "all isn't peaches and cream with us, either. The barons are far from licked, especially in the west." He changed the subject. "By the way, that banking deal went through in Pola. I was able to get control."

"Fine," Mayer chuckled. "You must be quite the richest man in the city. There is a certain stimulation in this financial game, Jerry, isn't there?"

"Uh huh," Jerry told him. "Of course, it doesn't hurt to have a marked deck."

"Marked deck?" the other frowned.

"It's handy that gold is the medium of exchange on Genoa," Jerry Kennedy said. "Especially in view of the fact that we have a machine on the ship capable of transmuting metals."

VI.

Leonid Plekhanov, Joseph Chessman, Barry Watson, Khan Reif and several of the Tulan army staff stood on a small knoll overlooking a valley of several square miles. A valley dominated on all sides but the sea by mountain ranges.

Reif and the three Earthlings were bent over a military map depicting the area. Barry Watson traced with his finger.

"There are only two major passes into this valley. We have this one, they dominate that."

Plekhanov was scowling, out of his element and knowing it. "How many men has Mynor been able to get together?"

Watson avoided looking into the older man's face. "Approximately half a million according to Hawkins' estimate. He flew over them this morning."

"Half a million!"

"Including the nomads, of course," Joe Chessman said. "The nomads fight more like a mob than an army."

Plekhanov was shaking his massive head. "Most of them will melt away if we continue to avoid battle. They can't feed that many men on the countryside. The nomads in particular will return home if they don't get a fight soon."

Watson hid his impatience. "That's the point, sir. If we don't break their power now, in a decisive defeat, we'll have them to fight again, later. And already they've got iron swords, the crossbow and even a few muskets. Given time and they'll all be so armed. Then the fat'll be in the fire."

"He's right," Joe Chessman said sourly.

Reif nodded his head. "We must finish them now, if we can. The task will be twice as great next year."

Plekhanov grumbled in irritation. "Half a million of them and something like forty thousand of our Tulans."

Reif corrected him. "Some thirty thousand Tulans, all infantrymen." He added, "And eight thousand allied cavalry only some of whom can be trusted." Reif's ten-year-old son came up next to him and peered down at the map.

"What's that child doing here?" Plekhanov snapped.

Reif looked into the other's face. "This is Taller Second, my son. You from First Earth have never bothered to study our customs. One of them is that a Khan's son participates in all battles his father does. It is his training."

Watson was pointing out features on the map again. "It will take three days for their full army to get in here." He added with emphasis, "In retreat, it would take them the same time to get out."

Plekhanov scowled heavily. "We can't risk it. If we were defeated, we have no reserve army. We'd have lost everything." He looked at Joe Chessman and Watson significantly. "We'd have to flee back to the *Pedagogue*."

Reif's face was expressionless.

Barry Watson looked at him. "We won't desert you, Reif, forget about that aspect of it."

Reif said, "I believe you, Barry Watson. You are a ... soldier."

Dick Hawkins' small biplane zoomed in, landed expertly at the knoll's foot. The occupant vaulted out and approached them at a half run.

Hawkins called as soon as he was within shouting distance. "They're moving in. Their advance cavalry units are already in the pass."

When he was with them, Plekhanov rubbed his hand nervously over heavy lips. He rumbled, "The cavalry, eh? Listen, Hawkins, get back there and dust them. Use the gas."

The pilot said slowly, "I have four bullet holes in my wings."

"Bullet holes!" Joe Chessman snapped.

Hawkins turned to him. "By the looks of things, MacBride's whole unit has gone over to the rebels. Complete with their double-barreled muskets. A full thousand of them."

Watson looked frigidly at Leonid Plekhanov. "You insisted on issuing guns to men we weren't sure of."

Plekhanov grumbled, "Confound it, don't use that tone of voice with me. We have to arm our men, don't we?"

Watson said, "Yes, but our still comparatively few advanced weapons shouldn't go into the hands of anybody but trusted citizens of the State, certainly not to a bunch of mercenaries. The only ones we can *really* trust even among the Tulans, are those that were kids when we first took over. The one's we've had time to indoctrinate."

"The mistake's made. It's too late now," Plekhanov said. "Hawkins go back and dust those cavalrymen as they come through the pass."

Reif said, "It was a mistake, too, to allow them the secret of the crossbow."

Plekhanov roared, "I didn't *allow* them anything. Once the crossbow was introduced it was just a matter of time before its method of construction got to the enemy."

"Then it shouldn't have been introduced," Reif said, his eyes unflinching from the Earthman's.

Plekhanov ignored him. He said, "Hawkins, get going on that dusting. Watson, pull what units we already have in this valley back through the pass we control. We'll avoid battle until more of their army has fallen away."

Hawkins said with deceptive mildness, "I just told you those cavalrymen have muskets. To fly low enough to use gas on them, I'd get within easy range. Point one, this is the only aircraft we've built. Point two, MacBride is probably dead, killed when those cavalrymen mutinied. Point three, I came on this expedition to help modernize the Texcocans, not to die in battle."

Plekhanov snarled at him. "Coward, eh?" He turned churlishly to Watson and Reif. "Start pulling back our units."

Barry Watson looked at Chessman. "Joe?"

Joe Chessman shook his head slowly. He said to Reif, "Khan, start bringing your infantry through the pass. Barry, we'll follow your plan of battle. We'll anchor one flank on the sea and concentrate what cavalry we can trust on the hills on the right. That's the bad spot, that right flank has to hold."

Plekhanov's thick lips trembled. He said in fury, "Is this insubordination?"

Reif turned on his heel and followed by young Taller and his staff hurried down the knoll to where their horses were tethered.

Chessman said to Hawkins, "If you've got the fuel, Dick, maybe it'd be a good idea to keep them under observation. Fly high enough, of course, to avoid gunfire."

Hawkins darted a look at Plekhanov, turned and hurried back to his plane.

Joe Chessman, his voice sullen, said to Plekhanov, "We can't afford any more mistakes, Leonid. We've had too many already." He said to Watson, "Be sure and let their cavalry units scout us out. Allow them to see that we're entering the valley too. They'll think they've got us trapped."

"They will have!" Plekhanov roared. "I countermand that order, Watson! We're withdrawing."

Barry Watson raised his eyebrows at Joe Chessman.

"Put him under arrest," Joe growled sourly. "We'll decide what to do about it later."

* * * * *

By the third day, Mynor's rebel and nomad army had filed through the pass and was forming itself into battle array. Rank upon rank upon rank.

The Tulan infantry had taken less than half a day to enter. They had camped and rested during the interval, the only action being on the part of the rival cavalry forces.

Now the thirty thousand Tulans went into their phalanx and began their march across the valley.

Joe Chessman, Hawkins, Roberts, Stevens and Khan Reif and several of his men again occupied the knoll which commanded a full view of the terrain. With binoculars and wrist radios from the *Pedagogue* they kept in contact with the battle.

Below, Barry Watson walked behind the advancing infantry. There were six divisions of five thousand men each, twenty-four foot *sarissas* stretched before their sixteen man deep line. Only the first few lines were able to extend their weapons; the rest gave weight and supplied replacements for the advanced lines' casualties. Behind them all the Tulan drums beat out the slow, inexorable march.

Cogswell, beside Watson with the wrist radio, said excitedly, "Here comes a cavalry charge, Barry. Reif says right behind it the nomad infantry is coming in." Cogswell cleared his throat. "All of them."

Watson held up a hand in signal to his officers. The phalanx ground to a halt, received the charge on the hedge of *sarissas*. The enemy cavalry wheeled and attempted to retreat to the flanks but were caught in a bloody confusion by the pressure of their own advancing infantry.

Cogswell, his ear to the radio, said, "Their main body of horse is hitting our right flank." He wet his lips. "We're outnumbered there something like ten to one. At least ten to one."

"They've got to hold," Watson said. "Tell Reif and Chessman that flank has to hold."

The enemy infantrymen in their hundreds of thousands hit the Tulan line in a clash of deafening military thunder. Barry Watson resumed his pacing. He signaled to the drummers who beat out another march. The phalanx moved forward slowly, and slowly went into an echelon formation, each division slightly ahead of the one following. Of necessity, the straight lines of the nomad and rebel front had to break.

The drums went *boom*, ah, *boom*, ah, *boom*, ah, *boom*.

The Tulan phalanx moved slowly, obliquely across the valley. The hedge of spears ruthlessly pressed the mass of enemy infantry before them.

The sergeants paced behind, shouting over the din. "Dress it up. You there, you've been hit, fall out to the rear."

"I'm all right," the wounded spearman snarled, battle lust in his voice.

"Fall out, I said," the sergeant roared. "You there, take his place."

The Tulan phalanx ground ahead.

One of the sergeants grinned wanly at Barry Watson as his men moved forward with the preciseness of the famed Rockettes of another era. "It's working," he said proudly.

Barry Watson snorted, "Don't give me credit. It belongs to a man named Philip of Macedon, a long ways away in both space and time."

Cogswell called, "Our right flank cavalry is falling back. Joe wants to know if you can send any support."

Watson's face went expressionless. "No," he said flatly. "It's got to hold. Tell Joe and the Khan it's got to hold. Suggest they throw in those cavalry units they're not sure of. The ones that threatened mutiny last week."

Joe Chessman stood on the knoll flanked by the Khan's ranking officers and the balance of the Earthmen. Natt Roberts was on the radio. He turned to the others and worriedly repeated the message.

Joe Chessman looked out over the valley. The thirty-thousand-man phalanx was pressing back the enemy infantry with the precision of a machine. He looked up the hillside at the point where the enemy cavalry was turning the right flank. Given cavalry behind the Tulan line and the battle was lost.

"O.K., boys," Chessman growled sourly, "we're in the clutch now. Hawkins!"

"Yeah," the pilot said.

"See what you can do. Use what bombs you have including the napalm. Fly as low as you can in the way of scaring their horses." He added sourly, "Avoiding scaring ours, if you can."

"You're the boss," Hawkins said, and scurried off toward his scout plane.

Joe Chessman growled to the others, "When I was taking my degree in primitive society and primitive military tactics, I didn't exactly have this in mind. Come on!"

It was the right thing to say. The other Earthmen laughed and took up their equipment, submachine guns, riot guns, a flame thrower, grenades, and followed him up the hill toward the fray.

Chessman said over his shoulder to Reif, "Khan, you're in the saddle. You can keep in touch with both Watson and us on the radio."

Reif hesitated only a moment. "There is no need for further direction of the battle from this point. A warrior is of more value now than a Khan. Come my son." He caught up a double-barreled musket and followed the Earthmen. The ten years old Taller scurried after with a revolver.

Natt Roberts said, "If we can hold their cavalry for only another half hour, Watson's phalanx will have their infantry pressed up against the pass they entered by. It took them three days to get through it, they're not going to be able to get out in hours."

"That's the idea," Joe Chessman said dourly, "Let's go."

VII.

Amschel Mayer was incensed.

"What's got into Buchwald and MacDonald?" he spat.

Jerry Kennedy, attired as was his superior in fur trimmed Genoese robes, signaled one of the servants for a refilling of his glass and shrugged.

"I suppose it's partly our own fault," he said lightly. He sipped the wine, made a mental note to buy up the rest of this vintage for his cellars before young Mannerheim or someone else did so.

"Our fault!" Mayer glared.

The old boy was getting decreasingly tolerant as the years went by, Kennedy decided. He said soothingly, "You sent Peter and Fred over there to speed up local development. Well, that's what they're doing."

"Are you insane!" Mayer squirmed in his chair. "Did you read this radiogram? They've squeezed out all my holdings in rubber, the fastest growing industry on the western continent. Why, millions are involved. Who do they think they are?"

Kennedy put down his glass and chuckled. "See here, Amschel, we're developing this planet by encouraging free competition. Our contention is that under such a socio-economic system the best men are brought to the lead and benefit all society by the advances they make."

"So! What has this got to do with MacDonald and Buchwald betraying my interests?"

"Don't you see? Using your own theory, you have been set back by someone more efficiently competitive. Fred and Peter saw an opening and, in keeping with your instructions, moved in. It's just coincidence that the rubber they took over was your property rather than some Genoese operator's. If you were open to a loss there, then if they hadn't taken over someone else could have. Possibly Baron Leonar or even Russ."

"That reminds me," Mayer snapped, "our Honorable Russ is getting too big for his britches in petroleum. Did you know he's established a laboratory in Amerus? Has a hundred or more chemists working on new products."

"Fine," Kennedy said.

"Fine! What do you mean? Dean is our man in petroleum."

"Look here, if Russ can develop the industry even faster than Mike Dean, let him go ahead. That's all to our advantage."

Mayer leaned forward and tapped his assistant emphatically on the knee. "Look here, yourself, Jerry Kennedy. At this stage we don't want things getting out of our hands. A culture is in the hands of those who control the wealth; the means of production, distribution, communication. Theirs is the real power. I've made a point of spacing our men about the whole planet. Each specializes, though not exclusively. Gunther is our mining man, Dean heads petroleum, MacDonald shipping, Buchwald textiles, Rykov steel, and so forth. As fast as this planet can assimilate we push new inventions, new techniques, often whole new sciences, into use. Meanwhile, you and I sit back and dominate it all through that strongest of power mediums, finance."

Jerry Kennedy nodded. "I wouldn't worry about old man Russ taking over Dean's domination of oil, though. Mike's got the support of all the *Pedagogue's* resources behind him. Besides, we've got to let these Genoese get into the act. The more the economy expands, the more capable men we need. As it is, I think we're already spread a little too thin."

Amschel Mayer had dropped the subject. He was reading the radiogram again and scowling his anger. "Well, this cooks MacDonald and Buchwald. I'll break them."

His assistant raised his eyebrows. "How do you mean?"

"I'm not going to put up with my subordinates going against my interests."

"In this case, what can you do about it? Business is business."

"You hold quite a bit of their paper, don't you?"

"You know that. Most of our team's finances funnel through my hands."

"We'll close them out. They've become too obsessed with their wealth. They've forgotten why the *Pedagogue* was sent here. I'll break them, Jerry. They'll come crawling. Perhaps I'll send them back to the *Pedagogue*. Make them stay aboard as crew."

Kennedy shrugged. "Well, Peter MacDonald's going to hate that. He's developed into quite a high liver-gourmet food, women, one of the swankiest estates on the eastern continent."

"Ha!" Mayer snorted. "Let him go back to ship's rations and crew's quarters."

A servant entered the lushly furnished room and announced, "Honorable Gunther calling on the Honorables Mayer and Kennedy."

Martin Gunther hurried into the room, for once his calm ruffled. "On the western continent," he blurted. "Dean and Rosetti. The Temple got them, they've been burned as witches."

Amschel Mayer shot to his feet. "That's the end," he swore shrilly. "Only in the west have the barons held out. I thought we'd slowly wear them down, take over their powers bit by bit. But this does it. This means we fight."

He spun to Kennedy. "Jerry, make a trip out to the *Pedagogue*. You know the extent of Genoa's industrial progress. Seek out the most advanced weapons this technology could produce."

Kennedy came to his own feet, shocked by Gunther's news. "But, Amschel, do you think it's wise to precipitate an intercontinental war? Remember, we've been helping to industrialize the west, too. It's almost as advanced as our continent. Their war potential isn't negligible."

"Nevertheless," Mayer snapped, "we've got to break the backs of the barons and the Temple monks. Get messages off to Baron Leonar and young Mannerheim, to Russ and Olderman. We'll want them to put pressure on their local politicians. What we need is a continental alliance for this war."

Gunther said, "Should I get in touch with Rykov? He's still over there."

Mayer hesitated. "No," he said. "We'll keep Nick informed but he ought to remain where he is. We'll still want our men in the basic positions of power after we've won."

"He might get hurt," Gunther scowled. "They might get him too, and we've only got six team members left now."

"Nonsense, Nick Rykov can take care of himself."

Jerry Kennedy was upset. "Are you sure about this war, chief? Isn't a conflict of this size apt to hold up our overall plans?"

"Of course not," Mayer scoffed. "Man makes his greatest progress under pressure. A major war will unite the nations of both the western continent and this one as nothing else could. Both will push their development to the utmost."

He added thoughtfully, "Which reminds me. It might be a good idea for us to begin accumulating interests in such industries as will be effected by a war economy."

Jerry Kennedy chuckled at him, "Merchant of death."

"What?"

"Nothing," Kennedy said. "Something I read about in a history book."

VIII.

At the decade's end, once again the representatives of the Genoese team were first in the *Ped-agogue's* lounge. Mayer sat at the officer's table, Martin Gunther at his right. Jerry Kennedy leaned against the ship's bar, sipping appreciatively at a highball.

They could hear the impact of the space boat from Texcoco when it slid into its bed.

"Poor piloting," Gunther mused. "Whoever's doing that flying doesn't get enough practice."

They could hear ports opening and then the sound of approaching feet. The footsteps had a strangely military ring.

Joe Chessman entered, followed immediately by Barry Watson, Dick Hawkins and Natt Roberts. They were all dressed in heavy uniform, complete with decorations. Behind them were four Texcocans, including Reif and his teen-age son Taller.

Mayer scowled at them in way of greeting. "Where's Plekhanov?"

"Leonid Plekhanov is no longer with us," Chessman said dourly. "Under pressure his mind evidently snapped and he made decisions that would have meant the collapse of the expedition. He resisted when we reasoned with him."

The four members of the Genoese team stared without speaking. Jerry Kennedy put down his glass at last. "You mean you had to restrict him? Why didn't you bring him back to the ship!"

Chessman took a chair at the table. The others assumed standing positions behind him. "I'm afraid we'll have to reject your views on the subject. Twenty years ago this expedition split into two groups. My team will accomplish its tasks, your opinions are not needed."

Amschel Mayer glared at the others in hostility. "You have certainly come in force this time."

Chessman said flatly, "This is all of us, Mayer."

"All of you! Where are Stevens, Cogswell, MacBride?"

Barry Watson said, "Plekhanov's fault. Lost in the battle that broke the back of the rebels. At least Cogswell and MacBride were. Stevens made the mistake of backing Plekhanov when the showdown came."

Joe Chessman looked sourly at his military chief. "I'll act as team spokesman, Barry."

"Yes, sir," Watson said.

"Broke the back of the rebels," Jerry Kennedy mused. "That opens all sorts of avenues, doesn't it?"

Chessman growled. "I suppose that in the past twenty years your team had no obstacles. Not a drop of blood shed. Come on, the truth. How many of your team has been lost?"

Mayer shifted in his chair. "Possibly your point is well taken. Dean and Rosetti were burned by the formerly dominant religious group. Rykov was killed in a fracas with bandits while he was transporting some gold." He added, musingly, "We lost more than half a million Genoese pounds in that robbery."

"Only three men lost, eh?"

Mayer stirred uncomfortably, then flushed in irritation at the other's tone. "Something has happened to Buchwald and MacDonald. They must be insane. They've broken off contact with me, are amassing personal fortunes in the eastern hemisphere."

Hawkins laughed abruptly. "Free competition," he said.

Chessman growled, "Let's halt this bickering and get to business. First let me introduce Reif, Texcocan State Army Chief of Staff and his son Taller. And these other Texcocans are Wiss and Fokin, both of whom have gone far in the sciences."

The Tulans shook hands, Earth style, but then stepped to the rear again where they followed the conversation without comment.

Mayer said, "You think it wise to introduce natives to the *Pedagogue*?"

"Of course," Chessman said. "Following this conference, I'm going to take Fokin and Wiss into the library. What're we here for if not to bring these people up to our level as rapidly as possible?"

"Very well," Mayer conceded grudgingly. "And now I have a complaint. When the *Pedagogue* first arrived we had only so many weapons aboard. You have appropriated more than half in the past two decades."

Chessman shrugged it off. "We'll return the greater part to the ship's arsenal. At this stage we are producing our own."

"I'll bet," Kennedy said. "Look, any of you fellows want a real Earthside whisky? When we were crewing this expedition, why didn't we bring someone with a knowledge of distilling, brewing and such?"

Mayer snapped at him, "Jerry, you drink too much."

"The hell I do," the other said cheerfully. "Not near enough."

Barry Watson said easily, "A drink wouldn't hurt. Why're we so stiff? This is the first get-together for ten years. Jerry, you're putting on weight."

Kennedy looked down at his admittedly rounded stomach. "Don't get enough exercise," he said, then reversed the attack. "You look older. Are your taking your rejuvenation treatments?"

Barry Watson grimaced. "Sure, but I'm working under pressure. It's been one long campaign."

Kennedy passed around the drinks.

Dick Hawkins laughed. "It's been one long campaign, all right. Barry has a house as big as a castle and six or eight women in his harem."

Watson flushed, but obviously without displeasure.

Martin Gunther, of the Genoese team, cocked his head. "Harem?"

Joe Chessman said impatiently, "Man adapts to circumstances, Gunther. The wars have lost us a lot of men. Women are consequently in a surplus. If the population curve is to continue upward, it's necessary that a man serve more than one woman. Polygamy is the obvious answer."

Gunther cleared his throat smoothly, "So a man in Barry's position will have as many as eight wives, eh? You must have lost a *good many* men."

Watson grinned modestly. "Everybody doesn't have that many. It's according to your ability to support them, and, also, rank has its privileges. Besides, we figure it's a good idea to spread the best seed around. By mixing our blood with the Texcocan we improve the breed."

Behind him, Taller, the Tulan boy, stirred, without notice.

* * * * *

Kennedy finished off his highball and began to build another immediately. "Here we go again. The big potatoes coming to the top."

Watson flushed. "What do you mean by that, Kennedy?"

"Oh, come off it, Barry," Kennedy laughed. "Just because you're in a position to push these people around doesn't make you the prize stud on Texcoco."

Watson elbowed Dick Hawkins to one side in his attempt to get around the table at the other.

Chessman rapped, "Watson! That's enough. Knock it off or I'll have you under arrest." The Texcocan team head turned abruptly to Mayer and Kennedy. "Let's stop this nonsense. We've come to compare progress. Let's begin."

The three members of the Genoese team glared back in antagonism, but then Gunther said grudgingly, "He's right. There is no longer amiability between us, so let's forget about it. Perhaps when the fifty years is up, things will be different. Now let's merely be businesslike."

'Well," Mayer said, "our report is that progress accelerates. Our industrial potential expands at a rate that surprises even us. In the near future we'll introduce the internal combustion engine. Our universities still multiply and are turning out technicians, engineers, scientists at an ever-quickening speed. In several nations illiteracy is practically unknown and per capita production increases almost everywhere." Mayer paused in satisfaction, as though awaiting the others to attempt to top his report.

Joe Chessman said sourly, "Ah, almost everywhere per capita production increases. Why *almost?*"

Mayer snapped, "Obviously, in a system of free competition, all cannot progress at once. Some go under."

"Whole nations?"

"Temporarily whole nations can receive setbacks as a result of defeat in war, or perhaps due to lack of natural resources. Some nations progress faster than others."

Chessman said, "The whole Texcocan State is one great unit. Everywhere the gross product increases. Within the foreseeable future the standard of living will be excellent."

Jerry Kennedy, an alcoholic lisp in his voice now, said, "You mean you've accomplished a planet-wide government?"

"Well, no. Not as yet," Chessman's sullen voice had an element of chagrin in it. "However, there are no strong elements left that oppose us. We are now pacifying the more remote areas."

"Sounds like a rather bloody program-especially if Barry Watson, here, winds up with eight women," Martin Gunther said.

Watson started to say something but Chessman held up a restraining hand. "The Texcocan State is too strong to be resisted, Gunther. It is mostly a matter of getting around to the more remote peoples. As soon as we bring in a new tribe, we convert it into a commune."

"Commune!" Kennedy blurted.

Joe Chessman raised his thick eyebrows at the other. "The most efficient socio-economic unit at this stage of development. Tribal society is perfectly adapted to fit into such a plan. The principal difference between a tribe and a commune is that under the commune you have the advantage of a State above in a position to give you the benefit of mass industries, schools, medical assistance. In return, of course, for a certain amount of taxes, military levies and so forth."

Martin Gunther said softly, "I recall reading of the commune system as a student, but I fail to remember the supposed advantages."

Chessman growled, "They're obvious. You have a unit of tens of thousands of persons. Instead of living in individual houses, each with a man working while the woman cooks and takes care of the home, all live in community houses and take their meals in messhalls. The children are cared for by trained nurses. During the season all physically capable adults go out en masse to work the fields. When the harvest has been taken in, the farmer does not hole up for the winter but is occupied in local industrial projects, or in road or dam building. The commune's labor is never idle."

Kennedy shuddered involuntarily.

Chessman looked at him coldly. "It means quick progress. Meanwhile, we go through each commune and from earliest youth, locate those members who are suited to higher studies. We bring them into State schools where they get as much education as they can assimilate-more than is available in commune schools. These are the Texcocans we are training in the sciences."

"The march to the anthill," Amschel Mayer muttered.

Chessman eyed him scornfully. "You amuse me, old man. You with your talk of building an economy with a system of free competition. Our Texcocans are sacrificing today but their children will live in abundance. Even today, no one starves, no one goes without shelter nor medical care." Chessman twisted his mouth wryly. "We have found that hungry, cold or sick people cannot work efficiently."

He stared challengingly at the Genoese leader. "Can you honestly say that there are no starving people in Genoa? No inadequately housed, no sick without hope of adequate medicine? Do you have economic setbacks in which poorly planned production goes amuck and depressions follow with mass unemployment?"

"Nevertheless," Mayer said with unwonted calm, "our society is still far ahead of yours. A mere handful of your bureaucracy and military chiefs enjoy the good things of life. There are tens of thousands on Genoa who have them. Free competition has its weaknesses, perhaps, but it provides a greater good for a greater number of persons."

Joe Chessman came to his feet. "We'll see," he said stolidly. "In ten years, Mayer, we'll consider the position of both planets once again."

"Ten years it is," Mayer snapped back at him.

Jerry Kennedy saluted with his glass. "Cheers," he said.

* * * * *

On the return to Genoa Amschel Mayer said to Kennedy, "Are you sober enough to assimilate something serious?"

"Sure, chief, of course."

"Hm-m-m. Well then, begin taking the steps necessary for us to place a few men on Texcoco in the way of, ah, intelligence agents."

"You mean some of our team?" Kennedy said, startled.

"No, of course not. We can't spare them, and, besides, there'd be too big a chance of recognition and exposure. Some of our more trusted Genoese. Make the monetary reward enough to attract their services." He looked at his lieutenants significantly. "I think you'll agree that it might not be a bad idea to keep our eyes on the developments on Texcoco."

* * * * *

On the way back to Texcoco, Barry Watson said to his chief, "What do you think of putting some security men on Genoa, just to keep tabs?"

"Why?"

Watson looked at his fingers, nibbled at a hangnail. "It just seems to me it wouldn't hurt any."

Chessman snorted.

Dick Hawkins said, "I think Barry's right. They can bear watching. Besides in another decade or so they'll realize we're going to beat them. Mayer's ego isn't going to take that. He'd go to just about any extreme to keep from losing face back on Earth."

Natt Roberts said worriedly, "I think they're right, Joe. Certainly it wouldn't hurt to have a few Security men over there. My department could train them and we'd ferry them over in this space boat."

"I'll make the decisions," Chessman growled at them. "I'll think about this. It's just possible that you're right though."

Behind them, Reif looked thoughtfully at his teen-age son.

IX.

Down the long palace corridor strode Barry Watson, Dick Hawkins, Natt Roberts, the aging Reif and his son Taller, now in the prime of manhood. Their faces were equally wan from long hours without sleep. Half a dozen Tulan infantrymen brought up their rear.

As they passed Security Police guards, to left and right, eyes took in their weapons, openly carried. But such eyes shifted and the guards remained at their posts. Only one sergeant opened his mouth in protest. "Sir," he said to Watson, hesitantly, "you are entering Number One's presence armed."

"Shut up," Natt Roberts rapped at him.

Reif said, "That will be all, sergeant."

The Security Police sergeant looked emptily after them as they progressed down the corridor.

Together, Watson and Reif motioned aside the two Tulan soldiers who stood before the door of their destination, and pushed inward without knocking.

Joe Chessman looked up wearily from his map and dispatch laden desk. For a moment his hand went to the heavy military revolver at his right but when he realized the identity of his callers, it fell away.

"What's up now?" he said, his voice on the verge of cracking.

Watson acted as spokesman. "It's everywhere the same. The communes are on the fine edge of revolt. They've been pushed too far; they've got to the point where they just don't give a damn. A spark and all Texcoco goes up in flames."

Reif said coldly, "We need immediate reforms. They've got to be pacified. An immediate announcement of more consumer goods, fewer State taxes, above all a relaxation of Security Police pressures. Given immediate promise of these, we might maintain ourselves."

Joe Chessman's sullen face was twitching at the right corner of his mouth. Young Taller made no attempt to disguise his contempt at the other's weakness in time of stress.

Chessman's eyes went around the half circle of them. "This is the only alternative? It'll slow up our heavy industry program. We might not catch up with Genoa as quickly as planned."

Watson gestured with a hand in quick irritation. "Look here, Chessman, don't we get through to you? Whether or not we build up a steel capacity as large as Amschel Mayer's isn't important now. Everything's at stake."

"Don't talk to me that way, Barry," Chessman growled truculently. "I'll make the decisions. I'll do the thinking." He said to Reif, "How much of the Tulan army is loyal?"

The aging Tulan looked at Watson before turning back to Joe Chessman. "All of the Tulan army is loyal-to me."

"Good!" Chessman pushed some of the dispatches on his desk aside, letting them flutter to the floor. He bared a field map. "If we crush half a dozen of the local communes ... crush them hard! Then the others..."

Watson said very slowly and so low as hardly to be heard, "You didn't bother to listen, Chessman. We told you, all that's needed is a spark."

Joe Chessman sat back in his chair, looked at them all again, one by one. Re-evaluating. For a moment the facial tic stopped and his eyes held the old alertness.

"I see," he said. "And you all recommend capitulation to their demands?"

"It's our only chance," Hawkins said. "We don't even know it'll work. There's always the chance if we throw them a few crumbs they'll want the whole loaf. You've got to remember that some of them have been living for twenty-five years or more under this pressure. The valve is about to blow."

"I see," Chessman grunted. "And what else? I can see in your faces there's something else."

The three Earthmen didn't answer. Their eyes shifted.

He looked to young Taller and then to Reif. "What else?"

"We need a scapegoat," Reif said without expression.

Joe Chessman thought about that. He looked to Barry Watson again.

Watson said, "The whole Texcocan State is about to topple. Not only do we have to give them immediate reform, but we're going to have to blame the past hardships and mistakes on somebody. Somebody has to take the rap, be thrown to the wolves. If not, maybe we'll all wind up taking the blame."

"Ah," Chessman said. His red-rimmed eyes went around them again, thoughtfully. "We should be able to dig up a few local chieftains and some of the Security Police heads."

They shook their heads. "It has to be somebody big," Natt Roberts said thickly, "a few of my Security Police won't do it."

Joe Chessman's eyes went to Reif. "The Khan is the highest ranking Texcocan of all," he said, finally. "The Khan and some Security Police heads would satisfy them."

Reif's face was as frigid as the Earthman's. He said, "I am afraid not, Joseph Chessman. You are Number One. It is your statue that is in every commune square. It is your portrait that hangs in every distribution center, every messhall, every schoolroom. You are the Number One-as you have so often pointed out to us. My title has become meaningless."

Joe Chessman spat out a curse, fumbled the gun into his hand and fired before the Tulan soldiers could get to him. In a moment they had wrested the weapon from his hand and had his arms pinioned. It was too late.

Reif had been thrown backward two paces by the blast of the heavy-calibered gun. Now he held a palm over his belly and staggered to a chair. He collapsed into it, looked at his son, let a wash of amusement pass over his face, said, "Khan," meaninglessly, and died.

Natt Roberts shrilled at Chessman, "You fool, we were going to give you a big, theatrical trial. Sentence you to prison and then, later, claim you'd died in your cell and smuggle you out to the *Pedagogue*."

Watson snapped to the guards, "Take him outside and shoot him."

The Tulans began dragging the snarling, cursing Chessman to the door.

Taller said, "A moment, please."

Watson, Roberts and Hawkins looked to him.

Taller said, "This perhaps can be done more effectively."

His voice was completely emotionless. "This man has killed both my father and grandfather, both of them Khans of Tula, heads of the most powerful city on all Texcoco, before the coming of you Earthlings."

The guards hesitated. Watson detained them with a motion of his hand.

Taller said, "I suggest you turn him over to me, to be dealt with in the traditional way of the People."

"No," Chessman said hoarsely. "Barry, Dick, Natt, send me back to the *Pedagogue*. I'll be out of things there. Or maybe Mayer can use me on Genoa."

They didn't bother to look in his direction. Roberts muttered savagely, "We told you all that was needed was a spark. Now you've killed the Khan, the most popular man on Texcoco. There's no way of saving you."

Taller said, "None of you have studied our traditions, our customs. But now, perhaps, you will understand the added effect of my taking charge. It will be a more ... profitable manner of using the downfall of this ... this power mad murderer."

Chessman said desperately, "Look, Barry, Natt, if you have to, shoot me. At least give me a man's death. Remember those human sacrifices the Tulans had when we first arrived? Can you imagine what went on in those temples? Barry, Dick-for old time's sake, boys..."

Barry Watson said to Taller, "He's yours. If this doesn't take the pressure off us, nothing will."

X.

At the end of the third decade, the Texcocan delegation was already seated in the *Pedagogue's* lounge when Jerome Kennedy, Martin Gunther, Peter MacDonald, Fredric Buchwald and three Genoese, Baron Leonar and the Honorables Russ and Modrin appeared.

The Texcocan group consisted of Barry Watson, Dick Hawkins and Natt Roberts to one side of him, Generalissimo Taller and six highly bemedaled Texcocans on the other.

Before taking a seat Barry Watson barked, "Where's Amschel Mayer? I've got some important points to cover with him."

"Take it easy," Kennedy slurred. "For that matter, where's Joe Chessman?"

Watson glared at the other. "You know where he is."

"That I do," Kennedy said. "He's purged, to use a term of yesteryear. At the rate you laddy-bucks are going, there won't be anything left of you by the time our half century is up." He snapped his fingers and a Genoese servant who'd been inconspicuously in the background, hurried to his side. "Let's have some refreshments here. What'll everybody have?"

"You act as though you've had enough already," Watson bit out.

Kennedy ignored him, insisted on everyone being served before he allowed the conversation to turn serious. Then he said, slyly, "I see we've been successful in apprehending all of your agents, or you'd know more of our affairs."

"Not all our agents," Watson barked. "Only those on your southern continent. What happened to Amschel Mayer?"

Peter MacDonald, who, with Buchwald, was for the first time attending one of the decade-end conferences, had been hardly recognized in his new girth by the Texcocan team. But his added weight had evidently done nothing to his keenness of mind. He said smoothly, "Our good Amschel is under arrest. Imprisoned, in fact." He shook his head, his double chin wobbling. "A tragedy."

"Imprisoned! By whom?" Taller scowled. "I don't like this. After all, he was your expedition's head man."

Barry Watson rapped, "Don't leave us there, MacDonald. What happened to him?"

MacDonald explained. "The financial and industrial empire he had built was overextended. A small crisis and it collapsed. Thousands of investors suffered. In brief, he was arrested and found guilty."

Watson was unbelieving. "There is nothing you could do? The whole team! Couldn't you bribe him out? Rescue him by force and get him back to the ship? With all the wealth you characters control —"

Jerry Kennedy laughed shortly. "We were busy bailing ourselves out of our own situations, Watson. You don't know what international finance can be. Besides, he dug his grave ...uh ... that is, he made his bed."

Kennedy signaled the servant for another drink, said, "Let's cut out this dismal talk. How about our progress reports?"

"Progress reports," Barry Watson said. "That's a laugh. You have agents on Texcoco, we have them on Genoa. What's the use of having these conferences at all?"

For the first time, one of the Genoese put in a word. Baron Leonar, son of the original Baron who had met with Amschel Mayer thirty years before, was a man in his mid-forties. He said quietly, "It seems to me the time has arrived when the two planets might profit by intercourse. Surely in this time one has progressed beyond the other in this field, but lagged in that. If I understand the mission of the *Pedagogue* it is to bring us to as high a technological level as possible in half a century. Already three decades have passed."

The Texcocans studied him thoughtfully, but Jerry Kennedy waved in negation with the hand that held his glass. "You don't get it, Baron. You see, the thing is we wanta find out what system is going to do the most the quickest. If we co-operate with Barry's gang, everything'll get all mixed up."

The Honorable Russ, now a wizened man of at least seventy, but still sharply alert, said, "However, Texcoco and Genoa might both profit."

Kennedy said happily, "What do we care? You gotta take the long view. What we're working out here is going to be used on half a million planets eventually." He tried to snap his fingers. "These two lousy planets don't count that much." He succeeded in snapping them this time. "Not that much."

Barry Watson said, "You're stoned, Kennedy."

"Why not?" Kennedy grinned. "Finally perfected a decent brandy. I'll have to send you a few cases, Barry."

"How would you go about that, Jerry?" Watson said softly.

"Shucks, man, our space lighter makes a trip to Texcoco every month or so. Gotta keep up with you boys. Maybe throw a wrench or so in the works once inna while."

Peter MacDonald said, "Shut up, Jerry. You talk too much."

"Don't talk to me that way. You'll find yourself having one helluva time floating that loan you need next month. How about another drink, everybody? This party's dead."

Watson said, "How about the progress reports? Briefly, we've all but completely united Texcoco. Minor setbacks have sometimes deterred us but the march of progress goes on. We —"

"Minor setbacks," Kennedy chortled. "Must of had to bump off five million of the poor slobs before that commune revolt was finished with."

Watson said coldly, "We always have a few reactionaries, religious fanatics, misfits, crackpots, malcontents to deal with. However, these are not important. Our industrial potential has finally begun to roll. We doubled steel production this year, will do the same next. Our hydro-electric installations tripled in the past two years. Coal production is four times higher, lumber production six times. We expect to increase grain harvest forty per cent next season. And —"

The Honorable Modrin put in gently, "Please, Honorable Watson, your percentage figures are impressive only if we know from what basis you start. If you produced but five million tons of steel last year, then your growth to ten million is very good but it is still not a considerable amount for an entire planet."

Buchwald said dryly, "If our agents are correct, Texcocan steel production is something like a quarter of our own. I assume your other basic products are at about the same stage of development."

Watson flushed. "The thing to remember is that our economy continues to grow each year. Yours spurts and stops, jerks ahead a few steps, then grinds to a halt or even retreats. Everything comes to a pause if you few on the top stop making a profit; all that counts in your economy is making money. Which reminds me, how in the world did you ever get out of that planet-wide depression you were in three years ago?"

Peter MacDonald grunted his disgust. "Planet-wide depression, indeed. A small recession. A temporary readjustment due to overextension in certain economic and financial fields."

From the other side of the table, Dick Hawkins laughed at him. "Where'd you pick up that line of gobbledygook, Peter?" he asked.

Peter MacDonald came to his feet. "I don't have to put up with this sort of impudence," he snapped.

Watson lurched to his own feet. "Nor do we have to listen to your snide cracks about the real progress Texcoco is making. We don't seem to be getting anywhere." He snapped to his associates, "Hawkins, Taller, Roberts! Let's go. Ten years from now, there'll be another story to tell. Even a blind man will see the difference."

They marched down the *Pedagogue's* corridor toward their space boat.

Kennedy called after them, "Ten years from now every family on Genoa'll have a car. Wait'll you see. Television, too. We're introducing TV next year. An' civil aviation. Be all over the place in two, three years —"

The Texcocans slammed the spaceport after them.

Kennedy sloshed some more drink into his glass. "Slobs can't stand the truth," he explained to the others.

XI.

With the exception of a few additional delegates composed of high-ranking Texcocan and Genoese political and scientific heads, the line-up at the end of forty years was the same as ten years earlier-except for the absence of Jerry Kennedy.

Extra tables had been set up, and chairs to accommodate the added numbers. To one side were the Genoese: Martin Gunther, Fredric Buchwald, Peter MacDonald, with such repeat delegates as Baron Leonar and the Honorables Modrin and Russ and half a dozen newcomers. On the other were Barry Watson, Dick Hawkins and Natt Roberts, Taller and such Texcocans as the scientists Wiss and Fokin, army heads, Security Police officials and other notables.

Note pads had been placed before each of them and both Watson and Gunther were equipped with gavels.

While chairs were still being shuffled, Barry Watson said over the table to Gunther, "Jerry?"

Martin Gunther shrugged "Jerry's indisposed. As a matter of fact, he's at one of the mountain sanitariums, taking a cure. He'll be all right."

"Good," Dick Hawkins said. "We've lost too many."

Watson pounded with his gavel. "Let's come to order. Gunther do you have anything to say in the way of preliminaries?"

"Not especially. I believe we all know where we stand, including the newcomers from Genoa and Texcoco. In brief, this is the fourth meeting of the Earth teams that were sent to these two planets to bring backward colonists to an industrialized culture. It would seem that we are both succeeding-possibly at different rates. Forty years have passed, ten remain to us."

For a moment there was silence.

Finally Roberts said, "Possibly you have already discovered this through your agents, but we have released the information on prolonging of life."

Peter MacDonald said wryly, "We, too, were pressured into such a step."

Baron Leonar said, "And why not?"

Taller, across the table from him, nodded.

Martin Gunther tapped twice on the table with his gavel. "The basic reason for our meeting is to report progress and to reconsider the possibilities of new elements having entered into the situation which might cause us to re-examine our policies. I think we already have a fairly good idea of each other's development." His voice went wry. "At least our agents do a fairly good job of reporting yours."

"And ours, yours," Watson rapped.

"However," MacDonald said, "now that we are drawing near the end of our half century, I think it becomes obvious that Amschel Mayer's original contention-that a freely competitive economy grows faster than one restricted by totalitarian bounds-has been proven."

Barry Watson snorted amusement. "Do you?" he said. "To the contrary, MacDonald. The proof is otherwise. On Genoa you still have comparative confusion. True enough, several of your nations, particularly those on your southern continent, are greatly advanced and with a high living and cultural standard-when times are good. But at the same time you have other whole peoples who are little, if any, better off, than when you arrived. On the western continent you even have a few feudalistic regimes that are probably worse off-mostly as a result of the wars you've crippled them with."

Natt Roberts said, his voice musing, "But even that isn't the important thing. The Co-ordinator sent us here to find a *method* of bringing backward cultures to industrialization. Have you got a blueprint to show him, when you return? Can you trace out the history of Genoa for this past half century and say, this war was necessary for progress-but that should have been avoided? Or is this whole *free competition* program of yours actually nothing but chaos which *sometimes* works out wonderfully for *some* nations, but actually destroys others? You have scorned our methods, our collectivized society-but when we return, we'll have a blueprint of how we arrived where we are."

Gunther banged the table with his gavel. "Just a moment. Is there any reason why we have to listen to these accusations when —"

Watson held up a hand, curtly, "Let us finish. If you have something to say, we'll gladly listen when we're through."

Gunther was flushed but he snapped, "Go ahead then, but don't think any of we Genoese are being taken in."

Watson said, "True enough, it took us a time to unite our people..."

"Time and blood," Peter MacDonald muttered.

"...But once underway the Texcocan State has moved on in a progression unknown in any of the Genoese nations. To industrialize a society you must reach a certain taking off point, a point where you have sufficient industry, particularly steel, sufficient power, sufficient scientists, technicians and skilled workers. Once that point has been reached you can move in almost a geometric progression. You build a steel mill and with the steel produced you build two more mills the following year, which in turn gives you the material for four the next year."

Buchwald grunted his disbelief.

Watson looked up and down the line of Genoese, the Earthmen as well as the natives. "On Texcoco we have now reached that point. We have a trained, eager population of over one billion persons. Our universities are turning out highly trained effectives at the rate of more than twenty million a year. We have located all the raw materials we will need. We are now under way." He looked at them in heavy amusement. "By the end of the next decade we will bury you."

Martin Gunther said calmly, "Are you through?"

"Yes. For the time," Watson nodded.

"Very well. Then this is *our* progress report. In the past forty years we have eliminated feudalism in all the more advanced countries. Even in the remote areas the pressures of our changing world are bringing them around. The populace of these countries will no longer stand to one side while the standard of living on the rest of Genoa grows so rapidly. On most of our planet, already the average family not only enjoys freedom but a way of life far in advance of that of Texcoco. Already modern housing and household appliances are everywhere. Already both land cars and aircraft are available to the majority. The nations have formed an Inter-Continental League of governments so that it is unlikely that war will ever touch us again. And this is merely a beginning. In ten years, continuing our freely competitive way of developing, all will be living on a scale that only the wealthy can afford today."

He came to an end and stared antagonistically at the Texcocans.

Taller said, "There seems to be no agreement."

Across the table from him the ancient Honorable Russ said, "It is difficult to measure. We seem to count refrigerators and privately owned automobiles. You seem to ignore personal standards and concentrate on steel tonnage."

The Texcocan scientist, Wiss, said easily, "Given the steel mills, and eventually automobiles and refrigerators will run off our assembly lines like water, and will be available for everyone, not just those who can afford to buy them."

"Hm-m-m, eventually," Peter MacDonald laughed nastily.

The atmosphere was suddenly hostile. Hostile beyond anything that had gone before in earlier conferences.

And then Martin Gunther said without inflection, "I note that you have removed from the *Pedagogue's* library the information dealing with nuclear fission."

"For the purpose of study," Dick Hawkins said smoothly.

"Of course," Gunther said. "Did you plan to return it in the immediate future?"

"I'm afraid our studies will take some time," Watson said flatly.

"I was afraid so," Gunther said. "Happily, I took the precaution of making microfilms of the material involved more than a year ago."

Barry Watson pushed his chair back. "We seem to have accomplished what was possible by this conference," he said. "If anything." He looked to right and left at his cohorts. "Let's go."

They came stiffly erect. Watson turned on his heel and started for the door.

As they left, Natt Roberts turned for a moment and said to Gunther, "One thing, Martin. During this next ten years you might consider whether or not half a century has been enough to accomplish our task. Should we consider staying on? I would think the Co-ordinator would accept any recommendation along this line that we might make."

The Genoese contingent looked after him, long after he was gone.

Finally Martin Gunther said, "Baron Leonar, I think it might be a good idea if you began putting some of your men to work on making steel alloys suitable for spacecraft. The way things are developing, perhaps we'll be needing them."

Buchwald and MacDonald looked at him unblinkingly.

XII.

It was fifty years to a day since the *Pedagogue* had first gone into orbit about Rigel. Five decades have passed. Half a century.

Of the original crew of the *Pedagogue*, six now gathered in the lounge of the spaceship. All of them had changed physically. Some of them softer to the point of flabbiness; some harder both of body and soul.

Barry Watson, Natt Roberts, Dick Hawkins, of the Texcocan team.

Martin Gunther, Peter MacDonald, Fredric Buchwald, of the Genoese.

The gathering wasn't so large as the one before. Only Taller and the scientist Wiss attended from Texcoco; only Baron Leonar and the son of Honorable Russ from Genoa.

From the beginning they stared with hostility across the conference table. Even the pretense of amiability was gone.

Watson rapped finally, "I am not going to dwell upon the measures you have been taking that can only be construed as military ones aimed eventually at the Texcocan State."

Martin Gunther laughed nastily. "Is your implication that your own people have not taken the same measures, in fact, inaugurated them?"

Watson said, "As I say, I have no intention of even discussing this. Surely we can arrive at no agreement. There is one point, however that we should consider on this occasion."

The corpulent Peter MacDonald wheezed, "Well, out with it!"

Natt Roberts said, "I mentioned the matter to you at the last meeting."

"Ah, yes," Gunther nodded. "Just as you left. We have considered it."

The Texcocans waited for him to go on.

"If I understand you," Gunther said, "you think we should reconsider returning to Terra City at this time."

"It should be discussed," Watson nodded. "Whatever the ...ah ...temporary difficulties between us, the original project of the *Pedagogue* is still our duty."

The three of the Genoese team nodded their agreement.

"And the problem becomes, have we accomplished completely what we set out to do? And, further, is it necessary, or at least preferable, for us to stay on and continue administration of the progress of the Rigel planets?"

They thought about it.

Buchwald said hesitantly, "It has been my own belief that Genoa is not quite ready for us to let loose the ...ah, reins. If we left now, I am not sure —"

Roberts said, "Same applies to Texcoco. The State has made fabulous strides, but I am not sure what would happen if we leaders were to leave. There might be a complete collapse."

Watson said, "We seem to be in basic agreement. Is a suggestion in order that we extend, for another twenty-five years, at least, this expedition's work?"

Dick Hawkins said, "The Office of Galactic Colonization —"

MacDonald said smoothly, "Will undoubtedly send out a ship to investigate. We shall simply inform them that things are not as yet propitious to our leaving, that another twenty-five years is in order. Since we are on the scene, undoubtedly our recommendation will be heeded."

Watson looked from one Earthman to the next. "We are in agreement?"

Each in turn nodded.

Peter MacDonald said, "And do you all realize that here we have a unique situation that might be exploited for the benefit of the whole race?"

They looked to him, questioningly.

"The dynamic we find in Genoa-and Texcoco, too, for that matter, though we disagree on so many fundamentals-is beyond that in the Solar System. These are new planets, new ambitions are alive. We have at our fingertips man's highest developments, evolved on Earth. But with this new dynamic, this freshness, might we not in time push even beyond old Earth?"

"You mean —" Natt Roberts said.

MacDonald nodded. "What particular of value is gained by our uniting Genoa and Texcoco with the so-called Galactic Commonwealth? Why not press ahead on our own? With the vigor of these new races we might well leave Earth far behind."

Watson mused, "Carrying your suggestion to the ultimate, who is to say that one day Rigel might not become the new center of the human race, rather than Sol?"

"A point well taken," Gunther agreed.

"No," Taller said softly.

The six Earthmen turned hostile eyes to him.

"This particular matter does not concern you, Generalissimo," Watson rapped at him.

Taller smiled his amusement at that and came to his feet.

"No," he said. "I am afraid that hard though it might be for you to give up the powers you have held so long, you Earthlings are going to have to return to Terra City, from whence you came."

Baron Leonar said in gentle agreement, "Obviously."

"What is this?" Watson rapped. "I'm not at all amused."

The Honorable Russ stood also. "There is no use prolonging this. I have heard you Earthlings say, more than once, that man adapts to preserve himself. Very well, we of Genoa and Texcoco are adapting to the present situation. We are of the belief that if you are allowed to remain in power we of the Rigel planets will be destroyed, probably in an atomic holocaust. In self-protection we have found it necessary to unite, we Genoese and Texcocans. We bear you no ill will, far to the contrary. However, it is necessary that you all return to Earth. You have impressed upon us the aforementioned truism that *man adapts* but in the *Pedagogue's* library I have found another that also applies. Power corrupts, and absolute power corrupts absolutely."

There were heavy automatics in the hands of Natt Roberts and Dick Hawkins. Barry Watson leaned back in his chair, his eyes narrow. "How'd you ever expect to get away with this sort of treason, Taller?"

Martin Gunther blurted, "Or you, Russ?"

Wiss, the Texcocan scientist, held his wrist radio to his mouth and said, "Come in now."

Dick Hawkins thumbed back the hammer of his hand gun.

"Hold it a minute, Dick," Barry Watson said. "I don't like this." To Taller he rapped, "What goes on here? Talk up, you're just about a dead man."

And it was then that they heard the scraping on the outer hull.

The six Earthmen looked at the overhead, dumfounded.

"I suggest you put up your weapons," Taller said quietly. "At this late stage I would hate to see further bloodshed."

In moments they heard the opening and closing of locks and footsteps along the corridor. The door opened and in stepped,

Joe Chessman, Amschel Mayer, Mike Dean, Louis Rosetti, and an emaciated Jerry Kennedy. Their expressions ran the gamut from sheepishness to blank haughtiness.

MacDonald bug-eyed. "Dean ... Rosetti ... the Temple priests burned you at the stake!"

They grinned at him, shamefaced. "Guess not," Dean said. "We were kidnaped. We've been teaching basic science, in some phony monastery."

Watson's face was white. "Joe," he said.

"Yeah," Joe Chessman growled. "You sold me out. But Taller and the Texcocans thought I was still of some use."

Amschel Mayer snapped, bitterly, "And now if you fools will put down your stupid guns, we'll make the final arrangements for returning this expedition to Terra City. Personally, I'll be glad to get away!"

Behind the five resurrected Earthmen were a sea of faces representing the foremost figures of both Texcoco and Genoa in every field of endeavor. At least fifty of them in all.

As though protectively, the eleven Earthmen ganged together at the far side of the messtable they'd met over so often.

Martin Gunther, his expression dazed, said, "I ... I don't —"

Taller resumed his spokesmanship. "From the first the most progressive elements on both Texcoco and Genoa realized the value of your expedition and have been in fundamental sympathy with the aims the *Pedagogue* originally had. Primitive life is not idyllic. Until man is free from nature's tyranny and has solved the basic problems of sufficient food, clothing, shelter, medical care and education for all, he is unable to realize himself. So we co-operated with you to the extent we found possible."

His smile was grim. "I am afraid that almost from the beginning, and on both planets, your very actions developed an ... underground, I believe you call it. Not an overt one, since we needed your assistance to build the new industrialized culture you showed us was possible. We even protected you against yourselves, since it soon became obvious that if left alone you'd destroy each other in your addiction to power."

Baron Leonar broke in, "Don't misunderstand. It wasn't until the past couple of decades that this *underground* which had sprung up independently on both planets, amalgamated."

Barry Watson blurted, "But Joe ... Chessman —" he refused to meet the eye of the man he'd condemned.

Taller said, "From the first you made no effort to study our customs. If you had, you'd have realized why my father allied himself to you after you'd killed Taller First. And why I did not take my revenge on Chessman after he'd killed Reif. A Khan's first training is that no personal emotion must interfere with the needs of the People. When you turned Joe Chessman over to me, I realized his education, his abilities were too great to destroy. We sent him to a mountain university and have used him profitably all these years. In fact, it was Chessman who finally brought us to space travel."

"That's right," Buchwald blurted. "You've got a spaceship out there. How could you possibly —?"

Taller said mildly, "There are but a handful of you, you could hardly keep track of two whole planets and all that went on upon them."

Amschel Mayer said bitingly, "All this can be gone over on our return to Terra City. We'll have a full year to explain to ourselves and each other why we became such complete idiots. I was originally head of this expedition-before my supposed friends railroaded me to prison-does anyone object if I take over again?"

"No," Joe Chessman growled.

The others shook their heads.

Taller said, "There is but one other thing. In spite of how you may feel at this moment of embarrassment, basically you have succeeded in your task. That is, you have brought Texcoco and Genoa to an industrialized culture. We hold various reservations about how you accomplished this. However, when you return to your Co-ordinator of Galactic Colonization, please inform him that we are anxious to receive his ambassadors. The term is *ambassadors* and we will expect to meet on a basis of equality. Surely in all Earth's millennia of social evolution man has worked out something better than either of your teams have built here. We should like to be instructed."

Dick Hawkins said stiffly, "We can instruct you on Earth's present socio-economic system."

"I am afraid we no longer trust you, Richard Hawkins. Send others-uncorrupted by power, privilege or great wealth."

* * * * *

When they had gone and the sound of their departing spacecraft had faded, Amschel Mayer snapped, "We might as well get underway. And cheer up, confound it, we have lots of time to contrive a reasonable report for the Co-ordinator."

Jerry Kennedy managed a thin grin, almost reminiscent of the younger Kennedy of the first years on Genoa. "Say," he said, "I wonder if we'll be granted a good long vacation before being sent on another assignment."

At least he'd got far enough to wind up with a personal interview. It's one thing doing up an application and seeing it go onto an endless tape and be fed into the maw of a machine and then to receive, in a matter of moments, a neatly printed rejection. It's another thing to receive an appointment to be interviewed by a placement officer in the Commissariat of Interplanetary Affairs, Department of Personnel. Ronny Bronston was under no illusions. Nine out of ten men of his age annually made the same application. Almost all were annually rejected. Statistically speaking practically nobody ever got an interplanetary position. But he'd made step one along the path of a lifetime ambition.

He stood at easy attention immediately inside the door. At the desk at the far side of the room the placement officer was going through a sheaf of papers. He looked up and said, "Ronald Bronston? Sit down. You'd like an interplanetary assignment, eh? So would I."

Ronny took the chair. For a moment he tried to appear alert, earnest, ambitious but not *too* ambitious, fearless, devoted to the cause, and indispensable. For a moment. Then he gave it up and looked like Ronny Bronston.

The other looked up and took him in. The personnel official saw a man of averages. In the late twenties. Average height, weight and breadth. Pleasant of face in an average sort of way, but not handsome. Less than sharp in dress, hair inclined to be on the undisciplined side. Brown of hair, dark of eye. In a crowd, inconspicuous. In short, Ronny Bronston.

The personnel officer grunted. He pushed a button, said something into his order box. A card slid into the slot and he took it out and stared gloomily at it.

"What're your politics?" he said.

"Politics?" Ronny Bronston said. "I haven't any politics. My father and grandfather before me have been citizens of United Planets. There hasn't been any politics in our family for three generations."

"Family?"

"None."

The other grunted and marked the card. "Racial prejudices?"

"I beg your pardon?"

"Do you have any racial prejudices? Any at all."

"No."

The personnel officer said, "Most people answer that way at first, these days, but some don't at second. For instance, suppose you had to have a blood transfusion. Would you have any objection to it being blood donated by, say, a Negro, a Chinese, or, say, a Jew?"

Ronny ticked it off on his fingers. "One of my greatgrandfathers was a French *colon* who married a Moroccan girl. The Moors are a blend of Berber, Arab, Jew and Negro. Another of my greatgrandfathers was a Hawaiian. They're largely a blend of Polynesians, Japanese, Chinese and Caucasians especially Portuguese. Another of my greatgrandfathers was Irish, English and Scotch. He married a girl who was half Latvian, half Russian." Ronny wound it up. "Believe me, if I had a blood transfusion from just anybody at all, the blood would feel right at home."

The interviewer snorted, even as he marked the card. "That accounts for three greatgrand-fathers," he said lightly. "You seem to have made a study of your family tree. What was the other one?"

Rocky said expressionlessly, "A Texan."

The secretary shrugged and looked at the card again. "Religion?"

"Reformed Agnostic," Ronny said. This one was possibly where he ran into a brick wall. Many of the planets had strong religious beliefs of one sort or another. Some of them had state religions and you either belonged or else.

"Is there any such church?" the personnel officer frowned.

"No. I'm a one-man member. I'm of the opinion that if there are any greater-powers-that-be They're keeping the fact from us. And if that's the way They want it, it's Their business. If and when They want to contact me-one of Their puppets dangling from a string-then I suppose They'll do it. Meanwhile, I'll wait."

The other said interestedly, "You think that if there is a Higher Power and if It ever wants to get in touch with you, It will?"

"Um-m-m. In Its own good time. Sort of a *don't call Me* , thing, *I'll call you* ."

The personnel officer said, "There have been a few revealed religions, you know."

"So they said, so they said. None of them have made much sense to me. If a Super-Power wanted to contact man, it seems unlikely to me that it'd be all wrapped up in a lot of complicated gobbledegook. It would all be very clear indeed."

The personnel officer sighed. He marked the card, stuck it back into the slot in his order box and it disappeared.

He looked up at Ronny Bronston. "All right, that's all."

Ronny came to his feet. "Well, what happened?"

The other grinned at him sourly. "Darned if I know," he said. "By the time you get to the outer office, you'll probably find out." He scratched the end of his nose and said, "I sometimes wonder what I'm doing here."

Ronny thanked him, told him good-by, and left.

* * * * *

In the outer office a girl looked up from a card she'd just pulled from her own order box. "Ronald Bronston?"

"That's right."

She handed the card to him. "You're to go to the office of Ross Metaxa in the Octagon, Commissariat of Interplanetary Affairs, Department of Justice, Bureau of Investigation, Section G."

In a lifetime spent in first preparing for United Planets employment and then in working for the organization, Ronny Bronston had never been in the Octagon Building. He'd seen photographs, Tri-Di broadcasts and he'd heard several thousand jokes on various levels from pun to obscenity about getting around in the building, but he'd never been there. For that matter, he'd never been in Greater Washington before, other than a long ago tourist trip. Population Statistics, his department, had its main offices in New Copenhagen.

His card was evidently all that he needed for entry.

At the sixth gate he dismissed his car and let it shoot back into the traffic mess. He went up to one of the guard-guides and presented the card.

The guide inspected it. "Section G of the Bureau of Investigation," he muttered. "Every day, something new. I never heard of it."

"It's probably some outfit in charge of cleaning the heads on space liners." Ronny said unhappily. He'd never heard of it either.

"Well, it's no problem," the guard-guide said. He summoned a three-wheel, fed the co-ordinates into it from Ronny's card, handed the card back and flipped an easy salute. "You'll soon know."

The scooter slid into the Octagon's hall traffic and proceeded up one corridor, down another, twice taking to ascending ramps. Ronny had read somewhere the total miles of corridors in the Octagon. He hadn't believed the figures at the time. Now he believed them. He must have traversed several miles before they got to the Department of Justice alone. It was another quarter mile to the Bureau of Investigation.

The scooter eventually came to a halt, waited long enough for Ronny to dismount and then hurried back into the traffic.

He entered the office. A neatly uniformed reception girl with a harassed and cynical eye looked up from her desk. "Ronald Bronston?" she said.

"That's right."

"Where've you been?" She had a snappy cuteness. "The commissioner has been awaiting you. Go through that door and to your left."

Ronny went through that door and to the left. There was another door, inconspicuously lettered *Ross Metaxa, Commissioner, Section G*. Ronny knocked and the door opened.

Ross Metaxa was going through a wad of papers. He looked up; a man in the middle years, sour of expression, moist of eye as though he either drank too much or slept too little.

"Sit down," he said. "You're Ronald Bronston, eh? What do they call you, Ronny? It says here you've got a sense of humor. That's one of the first requirements in this lunatic department."

Ronny sat down and tried to form some opinions of the other by his appearance. He was reminded of nothing so much as the stereotype city editor you saw in the historical romance Tri-Ds. All that was needed was for Metaxa to start banging on buttons and yelling something about tearing down the front page, whatever that meant.

Metaxa said, "It also says you have some queer hobbies. Judo, small weapons target shooting, mountain climbing —" He looked up from the reports. "Why does anybody climb mountains?"

Ronny said, "Nobody's ever figured out." That didn't seem to be enough, especially since Ross Metaxa was staring at him, so he added, "Possibly we devotees keep doing it in hopes that someday somebody'll find out."

Ross Metaxa said sourly, "Not *too* much humor, please. You don't act as though getting this position means much to you."

Ronny said slowly, "I figured out some time ago that every young man on Earth yearns for a job that will send him shuttling from one planet to another. To achieve it they study, they sweat, they make all out efforts to meet and suck up to anybody they think might help. Finally, when and if they get an interview for one of the few openings, they spruce up in their best clothes, put on their best party manners, present themselves as the sincere, high I.Q., ambitious young men that they are-and then flunk their chance. I decided I might as well be what I am."

Ross Metaxa looked at him. "O.K.," he said finally. "We'll give you a try."

Ronny said blankly, "You mean I've got the job?"

"That's right."

"I'll be damned."

"Probably," Metaxa said. He yawned. "Do you know what Section G handles?"

"Well no, but as for me, just so I get off Earth and see some of the galaxy."

* * * * *

Metaxa had been sitting with his heels on his desk. Now he put them down and reached a hand into a drawer to emerge with a brown bottle and two glasses. "Do you drink?" he said.

"Of course."

"Even during working hours?" Metaxa scowled.

"When occasion calls."

"Good," Metaxa said. He poured two drinks. "You'll get your fill of seeing the galaxy," he said. "Not that there's much to see. Man can settle only Earth-type planets and after you've seen a couple of hundred you've seen them all."

Ronny sipped at his drink, then blinked reproachfully down into the glass.

Metaxa said, "Good, eh? A kind of tequila they make on Deneb Eight. Bunch of Mexicans settled there."

"What," said Ronny hoarsely, "do they make it out of?"

"Lord only knows," Metaxa said. "To get back to Section G. We're Interplanetary Security. In short, Department Cloak and Dagger. Would you be willing to die for the United Planets, Bronston?"

That curve had come too fast. Ronny blinked again. "Only in emergency," he said. "Who'd want to kill me?"

Metaxa poured another drink. "Many of the people you'll be working with," he said.

"Well, *why* ? What will I be doing?"

"You'll be representing United Planets," Metaxa explained. "Representing United Planets in cases where the local situation is such that the folks you're working among will be teed off at the organization."

"Well, why are they members if they don't like the UP?"

"That's a good question," Metaxa said. He yawned. "I guess I'll have to go into my speech." He finished his drink. "Now, shut up till I give you some background. You're probably full of a lot of nonsense you picked up in school."

Ronny shut up. He'd expected more of an air of dedication in the Octagon and in such ethereal departments as that of Interplanetary Justice, however, he was in now and not adverse to picking up some sophistication beyond the ken of the Earth-bound employees of UP.

The other's voice took on a far away, albeit bored tone. "It seems that most of the times man gets a really big idea, he goes off half cocked. Just one example. Remember when the ancient Hellenes exploded into the Mediterranean? A score of different City-States began sending out colonies, which in turn sprouted colonies of their own. Take Syracuse, on Sicily. Hardly was she established than, bingo, she sent off colonists to Southern Italy, and they in turn to Southern France, Corsica, the Balearics. Greeks were exploding all over the place, largely without adequate plans, without rhyme or reason. Take Alexander. Roamed off all the way to India, founding cities and colonies of Greeks all along the way."

The older man shifted in his chair. "You wonder what I'm getting at, eh? Well, much the same thing is happening in man's explosion into space, now that he has the ability to leave the solar system behind. Dashing off half cocked, in all directions, he's flowing out over this section of the galaxy without plan, without rhyme or reason. I take that last back, he has reasons all right-some of the screwiest. Religious reasons, racial reasons, idealistic reasons, political reasons, altruistic reasons and mercenary reasons.

"Inadequate ships, manned by small numbers of inadequate people, setting out to find their own planets, to establish themselves on one of the numberless uninhabited worlds that offer themselves to colonization and exploitation."

Ronny cleared his throat. "Well, isn't that a good thing, sir?"

Ross Metaxa looked at him and grunted. "What difference does it make if it's good or not? It's happening. We're spreading our race out over tens of hundreds of new worlds in the most haphazard fashion. As a result, we of United Planets now have a chaotic mishmash on our hands. How we manage to keep as many planets in the organization as we do, sometimes baffles me. I suppose most of them are afraid to drop out, conscious of the protection UP gives against each other."

He picked up a report. "Here's Monet, originally colonized by a bunch of painters, writers, musicians and such. They had dreams of starting a new race" —Metaxa snorted —"with everybody artists. They were all so impractical that they even managed to crash their ship on landing. For three hundred years they were uncontacted. What did they have in the way of government by that time? A military theocracy, something like the Aztecs of Pre-Conquest Mexico. A matriarchy, at that. And what's their religion based on? That of ancient Phoenicia including plenty of human sacrifice to good old Moloch. What can United Planets do about it, now that they've become a member? Work away very delicately, trying to get them to at least eliminate the child sacrifice phase of their culture. Will they do it? Hell no, not if they can help it. The Head Priestess and her clique are afraid that if they don't have the threat of sacrifice to hold over the people, they'll be overthrown."

Ronny was surprised. "I'd never heard of a member planet like that. Monet?"

Metaxa sighed. "No, of course not. You've got a lot to learn, Ronny, my lad. First of all, what're Articles One and Two of the United Planets Charter?"

That was easy. Ronny recited. "Article One: *The United Planets organization shall take no steps to interfere with the internal political, socio-economic, or religious institutions of its member planets.* Article Two: *No member planets of United Planets shall interfere with the internal political, socioeconomic or religious institutions of any other member planet.* " He looked at the department head. "But what's that got to do with the fact that I was unfamiliar with even the existence of Monet?"

"Suppose one of the advanced planets, or even Earth itself," Metaxa growled, "openly discussed in magazines, on newscasts, or wherever, the religious system of Monet. A howl would go up among the liberals, the progressives, the do-gooders. And the howl would be heard on the other advanced planets. Eventually, the citizen in the street on Monet would hear about it and be affected. And before you knew it, a howl would go up from Monet's government. Why? Because the other planets would be interfering with her internal affairs, simply by discussing them."

"So what you mean is," Ronny said, "part of our job is to keep information about Monet's government and religion from being discussed at all on other member planets."

"That's right," Metaxa nodded. "And that's just one of our dirty little jobs. One of many. Section G, believe me, gets them all. Which brings us to your first assignment."

* * * * *

Ronny inched forward in his chair. "It takes me into space?"

"It takes you into space all right," Metaxa snorted. "At least it will after a few months of indoctrination. I'm sending you out after a legend, Ronny. You're fresh, possibly you'll get some ideas older men in the game haven't thought of."

"A legend?"

"I'm sending you to look for Tommy Paine. Some members of the department don't think he exists. I do."

"Tommy Paine?"

"A pseudonym that somebody hung on him way back before even my memory in this Section. Did you ever hear of Thomas Paine in American history?"

"He wrote a pamphlet during the Revolutionary War, didn't he?"

" 'Common Sense,' " Metaxa nodded. "But he was more than that. He was born in England but went to America as a young man and his writings probably did as much as anything to put over the revolt against the British. But that wasn't enough. When that revolution was successful he went back to England and tried to start one there. The government almost caught him, but he escaped and got to France where he participated in the French Revolution."

"He seemed to get around," Ronny Bronston said.

"And so does this namesake of his. We've been trying to catch up with him for some twenty years. How long before that he was active, we have no way of knowing. It was some time before we became aware of the fact that half the revolts, rebellions, revolutions and such that occur in the United Planets have his dirty finger stirring around in them."

"But you said some department members don't believe in his existence."

Metaxa grunted. "They're working on the theory that no one man could do all that Tommy Paine has laid to him. Possibly it's true that he sometimes gets the blame for accomplishments not his. Or, for that matter, possibly he's more than one person. I don't know."

"Well," Ronny said hesitantly, "what's an example of his activity?"

Metaxa picked up another report from the confusion of his desk. "Here's one only a month old. Dictator on the planet Megas. Kidnapped and forced to resign. There's still confusion but it looks as though a new type of government will be formed now."

"But how do they know it wasn't just some dissatisfied citizens of Megas?"

"It seems as though the kidnap vehicle was an old fashioned Earth-type helicopter. There were no such on Megas. So Section G suspects it's a possible Tommy Paine case. We could be wrong, of course. That's why I say the man's in the way of being a legend. Perhaps the others are right and he doesn't even exist. I think he does, and if so, it's our job to get him and put him out of circulation."

Ronny said slowly, "But why would that come under our jurisdiction? It seems to me that it would be up to the police of whatever planet he was on."

Ross Metaxa looked thoughtfully at his brown bottle, shook his head and returned it to its drawer. He looked at a desk watch. "Don't read into the United Planets organization more than there is. It's a fragile institution with practically no independent powers to wield. Every member planet is jealous of its prerogatives, which is understandable. It's no mistake that Articles One and Two are the basic foundation of the Charter. No member planet wants to be interfered with by any other or by United Planets as an organization. They want to be left alone.

"Within our ranks we have planets with every religion known to man throughout the ages. Everything ranging from primitive animism to the most advanced philosophic ethic. We have every political system ever dreamed of, and every socio-economic system. It can all be blamed on the crack-pot manner in which we're colonizing. Any minority, no matter how small-religious, political, racial, or whatever-if it can collect the funds to buy or rent a spacecraft, can dash off on its own, find a new Earth-type planet and set up in business.

'Fine. One of the prime jobs of Section G is to carry out, to enforce, Articles One and Two of the Charter. A planet with Buddhism as its state religion, doesn't want some die-hard Baptist missionary stirring up controversy. A planet with a feudalistic socio-economic systems doesn't want some hot-shot interplanetary businessman coming in with some big deal that would eventually cause the feudalistic nobility to be tossed onto the ash heap. A planet with a dictatorship doesn't want subversives from some democracy trying to undermine their institutions-and vice versa."

"And its our job to enforce all this, eh?" Ronny said.

"That's right," Metaxa told him sourly. "It's not always the nicest job in the system. However, if you believe in United Planets, an organization attempting to co-ordinate in such manner as it can, the efforts of its member planets, for the betterment of all, then you must accept Section G and Interplanetary Security."

Ronny Bronston thought about it.

Metaxa added, "That's why one of the requirements of this job is that you yourself be a citizen of United Planets, rather than of any individual planet, have no religious affiliations, no political beliefs, and no racial prejudices. You've got to be able to stand aloof."

'Yeah," Ronny said thoughtfully.

Ross Metaxa looked at his watch again and sighed wearily. "I'll turn you over to one of my assistants," he said. "I'll see you again, though, before you leave."

"Before I leave?" Ronny said, coming to his feet. "But where do I start looking for this Tommy Paine?"

"How the hell would I know?" Ross Metaxa growled.

* * * * *

In the outer office, Ronny said to the receptionist, "Commissioner Metaxa said for me to get in touch with Sid Jakes."

She said, "I'm Irene Kasansky. Are you with us?"

Ronny said, "I beg your pardon?"

She said impatiently, "Are you going to be with the Section? If you are, I've got to clear you with your old job. You were in statistics over in New Copenhagen, weren't you?"

Somehow it seemed far away now, the job he'd held for more than five years. "Oh, yes," he said. "Yes, Commissioner Metaxa has given me an appointment."

She looked up at him. "Probably to look for Tommy Paine."

He was taken aback. "That's right. How did you know?"

"There was talk. This Section is pretty well integrated." She grimaced, but on her it looked good. "One big happy family. High interdepartmental morale. That sort of jetsam." She flicked some switches. "You'll find Supervisor Jakes through that door, one to your left, two to your right."

He could have asked one *what* to his left and two *what* to his right, but evidently Irene Kasansky thought he had enough information to get him to his destination. She'd gone back to her work.

It was one turn to his left and two turns to his right. The door was lettered simply *Sidney Jakes*. He knocked and a voice shouted happily, "It's open. It's always open."

Supervisor Jakes was as informal as his superior. His attire was on the happy-go-lucky side, more suited for sports wear than a fairly high ranking job in the ultra-staid Octagon.

He couldn't have been much older than Ronny Bronston but he had a nervous vitality about him that would have worn out the other in a few hours. He jumped up and shook hands. "You must be Bronston. Call me Sid." He waved a hand at a typed report he'd been reading. "Now I've seen them all. They've just applied for entry to United Planets. Republic. What a name, eh?"

"What?" Ronny said.

"Sit down, sit down." He rushed Ronny to a chair, saw him seated, returned to the desk and flicked an order box switch. "Irene," he said, "do up a badge for Ronny, will you? You've got his code, haven't you? Good. Send it over. Bronze, of course."

Sid Jakes turned back to Ronny and grinned at him. He motioned to the report again. "What a name for a planet. Republic. Bunch of screw-balls, again. Out in the vicinity of Sirius. Based their system on Plato's *Republic*. Have to go the whole way. Don't even speak Basic. Certainly not. They speak Ancient Greek. That's going to be a neat trick, finding interpreters. How'd you like the Old Man?"

Ronny said, dazed at the conversational barrage, "Old Man? Oh, you mean Commissioner Metaxa."

"Sure, sure," Sid grinned, perching himself on the edge of the desk. "Did he give you that drink of tequila during working hours routine? He'd like to poison every new agent we get. What a character."

The grin was infectious. Ronny said carefully, "Well, I did think his method of hiring a new man was a little-cavalier."

"Cavalier, yet," Sid Jakes chortled. "Look, don't get the Old Man wrong. He knows what he's doing. He always knows what he's doing."

"But he took me on after only two or three minutes conversation."

Jakes cocked his head to one side. "Oh? You think so? When did you first apply for inter-planetary assignment, Ronny?"

"I don't know, about three years ago."

Jakes nodded. "Well, depend on it, you've been under observation for that length of time. At any one period, Section G is investigating possibly a thousand potential agents. We need men but qualifications are high."

He hopped down from his position, sped around to the other side of the desk and lowered himself into his chair. "Don't get the wrong idea, though. You're not in. You're on probation. Whatever the assignment the Old Man gave you, you've got to carry it out successfully before you're full fledged." He flicked the order-box switch and said, "Irene, where the devil's Ronny's badge?"

Ronny Bronston heard the office girl's voice answer snappishly.

"All right, all right," Jakes said. "I love you, too. Send it in when it comes." He turned to Ronny. "What *is* your assignment?"

"He wants me to go looking for some firebrand nicknamed Tommy Paine. I'm supposed to arrest him. The commissioner said you'd give me details."

* * * * *

Sid Jakes' face went serious. He puckered up his lips. "Wow, that'll be a neat trick to pull off," he said. He flicked the order-box switch again. Irene's voice snapped something before he could say anything and Sid Jakes grinned and said, "O.K., O.K., darling, but if this is the way you're going to be I won't marry you. Then what will the children say? Besides, that's not what I called about. Have ballistics do up a model H gun for Ronny, will you? Be sure it's adjusted to his code."

He flicked off the order box and turned back to Ronny. "I understand you're familiar with hand guns. It's in this report on you."

Ronny nodded. He was just beginning to adjust to this free-wheeling character. "What will I need a gun for?"

Jakes laughed. "Heavens to Betsy, you babe in the woods. Do you realize this Tommy Paine character has supposedly stirred up a couple of score wars, revolutions and revolts? Not to speak of having laid in his lap two or three dozen assassinations. He's a quick lad with a gun. A regular Nihilist."

"Nihilist?"

Jakes chuckled. "When you've been in this Section for a while, you'll be familiar with every screwball outfit man has ever dreamed up. The Nihilists were a European group, mostly Russian, back in the Nineteenth Century. They believed that by bumping off a few Grand Dukes and a Czar or so they could force the ruling class to grant reforms. Sometimes they were pretty ingenious. Blew up trains, that sort of thing."

"Look here," Ronny said, "what motivates this Paine fellow? What's he get out of all this trouble he stirs up?"

"Search me. Nobody seems to know. Some think he's a mental case. For one thing, he's not consistent."

"How do you mean?"

"Well, he'll go to one planet and break his back trying to overthrow, say, feudalism. Then, possibly after being successful, he goes to another planet and devotes his energies to establishing the same socio-economic system."

Ronny assimilated that. "You're one of those who believes he exists?"

"Oh, he exists all right, all right," Sid Jakes said happily. "Matter of fact, I almost ran into him a few years ago."

Ronny leaned forward. "I guess I ought to know about it. The more information I have, the better."

"Sure, sure," Jakes said. "This deal of mine was on one of the Aldebaran planets. A bunch of nature boys had settled there."

"Nature boys?"

"Um-m-m. Back to nature. The trouble with the human race is that it's got too far away from nature. So a whole flock of them landed on this planet. They call it Mother, of all things. They landed and set up a primitive society. Absolute stone age. No metals. Lived by the chase and by picking berries, wild fruit, that sort of thing. Not even any agriculture. Wore skins. Bows and arrows were the nearest thing they allowed themselves in the way of mechanical devices."

"Good grief," Ronny said.

"It was a laugh," Jakes told him. "I was assigned there as Section G representative with the UP organization. Picture it. We had to wear skins for clothes. We had to confine ourselves to two or three long houses. Something like the American Iroquois lived in before Columbus. Their society on Mother was based on primitive communism. The clan, the phratry, the tribe. Their religion was mostly a matter of knocking into everybody's head that any progress was taboo. Oh, it was great."

"Well, were they happy?"

"What's happiness? I suppose they were as happy as anybody ever averages. Frankly, I didn't mind the assignment. Lots of fishing, lots of hunting."

Ronny said, "Well, where does Tommy Paine come in?"

"He snuck up on us. Started way back in the boondocks away from any of the larger primitive settlements. Went around putting himself over as a holy man. Cured people of various things from gangrene to eye diseases. Given antibiotics and such, you can imagine how successful he was."

"Well, what harm did he do?"

"I didn't say he did any harm. But in that manner he made himself awfully popular. Then he'd pull some trick like showing them how to smelt iron, and distribute some corn and wheat seed around and plant the idea of agriculture. The local witch doctors would try to give him a hard time, but the people figured he was a holy man."

"Well, what happened finally?" Ronny wasn't following too well.

"Communications being what they were, before he'd been discovered by the central organization-they had a kind of Council of Tribes which met once a year-he'd planted so many ideas that they couldn't be stopped. The young people'd never go back to flint knives, once introduced to iron. We went looking for friend Tommy Paine, but he got wind of it and took off. We even found where he'd hidden his little space cruiser. Oh, it was Paine, all right, all right."

"But what harm did he do? I don't understand," Ronny scowled.

"He threw the whole shebang on its ear. Last I heard, the planet had broken up into three main camps. They were whaling away at each other like the Assyrians and Egyptians. Iron weapons, chariots, domesticated horses. Agriculture was sweeping the planet. Population was exploding. Men were making slaves out of each other, to put them to work. Oh, it was a mess from the viewpoint of the original nature boys."

A red light flickered on his desk and Sid Jakes opened a delivery drawer and dipped his hand into it. It emerged with a flat wallet. He tossed it to Ronny Bronston.

"Here you are. Your badge."

Ronny opened the wallet and examined it. He'd never seen one before, but for that matter he'd never heard of Section G before that morning. It was a simple enough bronze badge. It said on it, merely, *Ronald Bronston, Section G, Bureau of Investigation, United Planets* .

Sid Jakes explained. "You'll get co-operation with that through the Justice Department anywhere you go. We'll brief you further on procedure during indoctrination. You in turn, of course, are to co-operate with any other agent of Section G. You're under orders of anyone with" —his hand snaked into a pocket and emerged with a wallet similar to Ronny's —"a silver badge, carried by a First Grade Agent, or a gold one of Supervisor rank."

Ronny noted that his badge wasn't really bronze. It had a certain sheen, a brightness.

Jakes said, "Here, look at this." He tossed his own badge to the new man. Ronny looked down at it in surprise. The gold had gone dull.

Jakes laughed. "Now give me yours."

Ronny got up and walked over to him and handed it over. As soon as the other man's hand touched it, the bronze lost its sheen.

Jakes handed it back. "See, it's tuned to you alone," he said. "And mine is tuned to my code. Nobody can swipe a Section G badge and impersonate an agent. If anybody ever shows you a badge that doesn't have its sheen, you know he's a fake. Neat trick, eh?"

"Very neat," Ronny admitted. He returned the other's gold badge. "Look, to get back to this Tommy Paine."

But the red light flickered again and Jakes brought forth from the delivery drawer a hand gun complete with shoulder harness. "Nasty weapon," he said. "But we'd better go on down to the armory and show you its workings."

He stood up. "Oh, yes, don't let me forget to give you a communicator. A real gizmo. About as big as a woman's vanity case. Puts you in immediate contact with the nearest Section G office, no matter how near or far away it is. Or, if you wish, in contact with our offices here in the Octagon. Very neat trick."

He led Ronny from his office and down the corridors beyond to an elevator. He said happily, "This is a crazy outfit, this Section G. You'll probably love it. Everybody does."

* * * * *

Ronny learned to love Section G —in moderation.

He was initially taken aback by the existence of the organization at all. He'd known, of course, of the Department of Justice and even of the Bureau of Investigation, but Section G was hush-hush and not even United Planets publications ever mentioned it.

The problems involved in remaining hush-hush weren't as great as all that. The very magnitude of the UP which involved more than two thousand member planets, allowed of departments and bureaus hidden away in the endless stretches of red tape.

In fact, although Ronny Bronston had spent the better part of his life, thus far, in studying for a place in the organization, and then working in the Population Statistics Department for some years, he was only now beginning to get the over-all picture of the workings of the mushrooming, chaotic United Planets organization.

It was Earth's largest industry by far. In fact, for all practical purposes it was her only major industry. Tourism, yes, but even that, in a way, was related to the United Planets organization. Millions of visitors whose ancestors had once emigrated from the mother planet, streamed back in racial nostalgia. Streamed back to see the continents and oceans, the Arctic and the Antarctic, the Amazon River and Mount Everest, the Sahara and New York City, the ruins of Rome and Athens, the Vatican, the Louvre and the Hermitage.

But the populace of Earth, in its hundreds of millions were largely citizens of United Planets and worked in the organization and with its auxiliaries such as the Space Forces.

Section G? To his surprise, Ronny found that Ross Metaxa's small section of the Bureau of Investigation seemed almost as great a secret within the Bureau as it was to the man in the street. At one period, Ronny wondered if it were possible that this was a department which had been lost in the wilderness of boondoggling that goes on in any great bureaucracy. Had Section G been set up a century or so ago and then forgotten by those who had originally thought there was a need for it? In the same way that it is usually more difficult to get a statute off the lawbooks than it was originally to pass it, in the same manner eliminating an office, with its employees can prove more difficult than originally establishing it.

But that wasn't it. In spite of the informality, the unconventional brashness of its personnel on all levels, and the seeming chaos in which its tasks were done, Section G was no make-work project set up to provide juicy jobs for the relatives of high ranking officials. To the contrary, it didn't take long in the Section before anybody with open eyes could see that Ross Metaxa was privy to the decisions made by the upper echelons of UP.

Ronny Bronston came to the conclusion that the appointment he'd received was putting him in a higher bracket of the UP hierarchy than he'd at first imagined.

His indoctrination course was a strain such as he'd never known in school years. Ross Metaxa was evidently of the opinion that a man could assimilate concentrated information at a rate several times faster than any professional educator ever dreamed possible. No threats were made, but Ronny realized that he could be dropped even more quickly than he'd seemed to have been taken on. There were no classes, to either push or retard the rate of study. He worked with a series of tutors, and pushed himself. The tutors were almost invariably Section G agents, temporarily in Greater Washington between assignments, or for briefing on this phase or that of their work.

Even as he studied, Ronny Bronston kept the eventual assignment, at which he was to prove himself, in mind. He made a point of inquiring of each agent he met, about Tommy Paine.

The name was known to all, but no two reacted in the same manner. Several of them even brushed the whole matter aside as pure legend. *Nobody* could accomplish all the trouble that Tommy Paine had supposedly stirred up.

To one of these, Ronny said plaintively, "See here, the Old Man believes in him, Sid Jakes believes in him. My final appointment depends on arresting him. How can I ever secure this job, if I'm chasing a myth?"

The other shrugged. "Don't ask me. I've got my own problems. O.K., now, let's run over this question of Napoleonic law. There are at least two hundred planets that base their legal system on it."

But the majority of his fellow employees in Section G had strong enough opinions on the interplanetary firebrand. Three or four even claimed to have seen him fleetingly, although no two descriptions jibed. That, of course, could be explained. The man could resort to plastic surgery and other disguise.

Theories there were in plenty, some of them going back long years, and some of them pure fable.

* * * * *

"Look," Ronny said in disgust one day after a particularly unbelievable siege with two agents recently returned from a trouble spot in a planetary system that involved three aggressive worlds which revolved about the same sun. "Look, it's impossible for one man to accomplish all this. He's blamed for half the *coups d'états* , revolts and upheavals that have taken place for the past quarter century. It's obvious nonsense. Why, a revolutionist usually spends the greater part of his life toppling a government. Then, once it's toppled, he spends the rest of his life trying to set up a new government-and he's usually unsuccessful."

One of the others was shaking his head negatively. "You don't understand this Tommy Paine's system, Bronston."

"You sure don't," the other agent, a Nigerian, grinned widely. "I've been on planets where he'd operated."

Ronny leaned forward. The three of them were having a beer in a part of the city once called Baltimore. "You have?" he said. "Tell me about it, eh? The more background I get on this guy, the better."

"Sure. And this'll give you an idea of how he operates, how he can get so much trouble done. Well, I was on this planet Goshen, understand? It had kind of a strange history. A bunch of colonists went out there, oh, four or five centuries ago. Pretty healthy expedition, as such outfits go. Bright young people, lots of equipment, lots of know-how and books. Well, through sheer bad luck everything went wrong from the beginning. Everything. Before they got set up at all they had an explosion that killed off all their communications technicians. They lost contact with the outside. O.K. Within a couple of centuries they'd gotten into a state of chattel slavery. Pretty well organized, but static. Kind of an Athenian Democracy on top, a hierarchy, but nineteen people out of twenty were slaves, and I mean real slaves, like animals. They were at this stage when a scout ship from the UP Space Forces discovered them and, of course, they joined up."

"Where does Tommy Paine come in?" Ronny said. He signaled to a waiter for more beer.

"He comes in a few years later. I was the Section G agent on Goshen, understand? No planet was keener about Articles One and Two of the UP Charter. The hierarchy understood well enough that if their people ever came to know about more advanced socio-economic systems it'd be the end of Goshen's Golden Age. So they allowed practically no intercourse. No contact whatsoever between UP personnel and anyone outside the upper class, understand? All right. That's where Tommy Paine came in. It couldn't have taken him more than a couple of months at most."

Ronny Bronston was fascinated. "What'd he do?"

"He introduced the steam engine, and then left."

Ronny was looking at him blankly. "Steam engine?"

"That and the fly shuttle and the spinning jenny," the Nigerian said. "That Goshen hierarchy never knew what hit them."

Ronny was still blank. The waiter came up with the steins of beer, and Ronny took one and drained half of it without taking his eyes from the storyteller.

The other agent took it up. "Don't you see? Their system was based on chattel slavery, hand labor. Given machinery and it collapses. Chattel slavery isn't practical in a mechanized society. Too expensive a labor force, for one thing. Besides, you need an educated man and one with some initiative-qualities that few slaves possess-to run an industrial society."

Ronny finished his beer. "Smart cooky, isn't he?"

"He's smart all right. But I've got a still better example of his fouling up a whole planetary socio-economic system in a matter of weeks. A friend of mine was working on a planet with a highly-developed feudalism. Barons, lords, dukes, counts and no-accounts, all stashed safely away in castles and fortresses up on the top of hills. The serfs down below did all the work in the fields, provided servants, artisans and foot soldiers for the continual fighting that the aristocracy carried on. Very similar to Europe back in the Dark Ages."

"So?" Ronny said. "I'd think that'd be a deal that would take centuries to change."

The Section G agent laughed. "Tommy Paine stayed just long enough to introduce gunpowder. That was the end of those impregnable castles up on the hills."

"What gets me," Ronny said slowly, "is his motivation."

The other two both grunted agreement to that.

* * * * *

Toward the end of his indoctrination studies, Ronny appeared one morning at the Octagon Section G offices and before Irene Kasansky. Watching her fingers fly, listening to her voice rapping and snapping, O.K.-ing and rejecting, he came to the conclusion that automation could go just so far in office work and then you were thrown back on the hands of the efficient secretary. Irene was a one-woman office staff.

She looked up at him. "Hello, Ronny. Thought you'd be off on your assignment by now. Got any clues on Tommy Paine?"

"No," he said. "That's why I'm here. I wanted to see the commissioner."

"About what?" She flicked a switch. When a light flickered on one of her order boxes, she said into it, "No," emphatically, and turned back to him.

"He said he wanted to see me again before I took off."

She fiddled some more, finally said, "All right, Ronny. Tell him he's got time for five minutes with you."

"Five minutes!"

"Then he's got an appointment with the Commissioner of Interplanetary Culture," she said. "You'd better hurry along."

Ronny Bronston retraced the route of his first visit here. How long ago? It already seemed ages since his probationary appointment. Your life changed fast when you were in Section G.

Ross Metaxa's brown bottle, or its twin, was sitting on his desk and he was staring at it glumly. He looked up and scowled.

"Ronald Bronston," Ronny said. "Irene Kasansky told me to say I could have five minutes with you, then you have an appointment with the Commissioner of Interplanetary Culture."

"I remember you," Metaxa said. "Have a drink. Interplanetary Culture, ha! The Xanadu Folk Dance Troupe. They dance nude. They've been touring the whole UP. Roaring success everywhere, obviously. Now they're assigned to Virtue, a planet settled by a bunch of Fundamentalists. They want the troupe to wear Mother Hubbards. The Xanadu outfit is in a tizzy. They've been insulted. They claim they're the most modest members of UP, that nudity has nothing to do with modesty. The government of Virtue said that's fine but they wear Mother Hubbards or they don't dance. Xanadu says it'll withdraw from United Planets."

Ronny Bronston said painfully, "Why not let them?"

Ross Metaxa poured himself a Denebian tequila, offered his subordinate a drink again with a motion of the bottle. Ronny shook his head.

Metaxa said, "If we didn't take steps to soothe these things over, there wouldn't be any United Planets. In any given century every member in the organization threatens to resign at least once. Even Earth. And then what'd happen? You'd have interplanetary war before you knew it. What'd you want, Ronny?"

"I'm about set to take up my search for this Tommy Paine."

"Ah, yes, Tommy Paine. If you catch him, there are a dozen planets where he'd be eligible for the death sentence."

Ronny cleared his throat. "There must be. What I wanted was the file on him, sir."

"File?"

"Yes, sir. I've got to the point where I want to cram up on everything we have on him. So far, all I've got is verbal information from individual agents and from Supervisor Jakes."

"Don't be silly, Ronny. There isn't any file on Tommy Paine."

Ronny just looked at the other.

Ross Metaxa said impatiently, "The very knowledge of the existence of the man is top secret. Isn't that obvious? Suppose some reporter got the story and printed it. If our member planets knew there was such a man and that we haven't been able to scotch him, why they'd drop out of UP so fast the computers couldn't keep up with it. There's not one planet in ten that feels secure enough to lay itself open to subversion. Why some of our planets are so far down the ladder of social evolution they live under primitive tribal society; their leaders, their wise men and witch-doctors, whatever you call them, are scared someone will come along and establish chattel slavery. Those planets that have a system based on slavery are scared to death of developing feudalism, and those that have feudalism are afraid of *creeping capitalism* . Those with an anarchistic basis-and we have several-are afraid of being subverted to statism, and those who have a highly developed government are afraid of anarchism. The socio-economic systems based on private ownership of property hate the very idea of socialism or communism, and vice versa, and those planets with state capitalism hate them both."

He glared at Ronny. "What do you think the purpose of this Section is, Bronston? Our job is to keep our member planets from being afraid of each other. If they found that Tommy Paine and his group, if he's got a group, were buzzing through the system subverting everything they can foul up, they'd drop out of UP and set up quarantines that a space mite couldn't get through. No sir, there is no file on Tommy Paine and there never will be. And if any news of him spreads to the outside, this Section will emphatically deny he exists. I hope that's clear."

"Well, yes sir," Ronny said. The commissioner had been all but roaring toward the end.

The order box clicked on Ross Metaxa's desk and he said loudly, "What?"

"Don't yell at me," Irene snapped back. "Ronny's five minutes are up. You've got an appointment. I'm getting tired of this job. It's a mad-house. I'm going to quit and get a job with Interplanetary Finance."

"Oh, yeah." Ross snarled back. "That's what you think. I've taken measures. Top security. I've warned off every Commissioner in UP. You can't get away from me until you reach retirement age. Although I don't know why I care. I hate nasty tempered women."

"Huh!" she snorted and clicked off.

"There's a woman for you," Ross Metaxa growled at Ronny. "It's too bad she's indispensable. I'd love to fire her. Look, you go in and see Sid Jakes. Seems to me he said something about Tommy Paine this morning. Maybe it's a lead." He came to his feet. "So long and good luck, Ronny. I feel optimistic about you. I think you'll get this Paine troublemaker."

Which was more than Ronny Bronston thought.

Sid Jakes already had a visitor in his office, which didn't prevent him from yelling, "It's open," when Ronny Bronston knocked.

He bounced from his chair, came around the desk and shook hands enthusiastically. "Ronny!" he said, his tone implying they were favorite brothers for long years parted. "You're just in time."

Ronny took in the office's other occupant appreciatively. She was a small girl, almost tiny. He estimated her to be at least half Chinese, or maybe Indo-Chinese, the rest probably European or North American.

She evidently favored her Asiatic blood, her dress was traditional Chinese, slit almost to the thigh Shanghai style.

Sid Jakes said, "Tog Lee Chang Chu-Ronny Bronston. You'll be working together. Bloodhounding old Tommy Paine. A neat trick if you can pull it off. Well, are you all set to go?"

Ronny mumbled something to the girl in the way of amenity, then looked back at the supervisor. "Working together?" he said.

"That's right. Lucky you, eh?"

Tog Lee Chang Chu said demurely, "Possibly Mr. Bronston objects to having a female assistant."

Sid Jakes snorted, and hurried around his desk to resume his seat. "Does he look crazy? Who'd object to having a cutey like you around day in and day out? Call him Ronny. Might as well get used to it. Two of you'll be closer than man and wife."

"Assistant?" Ronny said, bewildered. "What do I need an assistant for?" He turned his eyes to the girl. "No reflection on you, Miss ... ah, Tog."

Sid Jakes laughed easily. "Section G operatives always work in pairs, Ronny. Especially new agents. The advantages will come home to you as you go along. Look on Tog Lee Chang Chu as a secretary, a man Friday. This isn't her first assignment, of course. You'll find her invaluable."

The supervisor plucked a card from an order box. "Now here's the dope. Can you leave within four hours? There's a UP Space Forces cruiser going to Merlini, they can drop you off at New Delos. Fastest way you could possibly get there. The cruiser takes off from Neuve Albuquerque in, let's see, three hours and forty-five minutes."

"New Delos?" Ronny said, taking his eyes from the girl and trying to catch up with the grasshopper-like conversation of his superior.

"New Delos it is," Jakes said happily. "With luck, you might catch him before he can get off the planet." He chuckled at the other's expression. "Look alive, Ronny! The quarry is flushed and on the run. Tommy Paine's just assassinated the Immortal God-King of New Delos. A neat trick, eh?"

* * * * *

The following hours were chaotic. There was no indication of how long a period he'd be gone. For all he knew, it might be years. For that matter, he might never return to Earth. This Ronny

Bronston had realized before he ever applied for an interplanetary appointment. Mankind was exploding through this spiral arm of the galaxy. There was a racial enthusiasm about it all. Man's destiny lay out in the stars, only a laggard stayed home of his own accord. It was the ambition of every youth to join the snowballing avalanche of man into the neighboring stars.

It took absolute severity by Earth authorities to prevent the depopulation of the planet. But someone had to stay to administer the ever more complicated racial destiny. Earth became a clearing house for a thousand cultures, attempting, with only moderate success, to co-ordinate her widely spreading children. She couldn't afford to let her best seed depart. Few there were, any more, allowed to emigrate from Earth. New colonies drew their immigrants from older ones.

Lucky was the Earthling able to find service in interplanetary affairs, in any of the thousands of tasks that involved journey between member planets of UP. Possibly one hundredth of the population at one time or another, and for varying lengths of time, managed it.

Ronny Bronston was lucky and knew it. The thing now was to pull off this assignment and cinch the appointment for good.

He packed in a swirl of confusion. He phoned a relative who lived in the part of town once known as Richmond, explained the situation and asked that the other store his things and dispose of the apartment he'd been occupying.

Luckily, the roof of his apartment building was a copter-cab pickup point and he was able to hustle over to the shuttleport in a matter of a few minutes.

He banged into the reservations office, hurried up to one of the windows and said into the screen, "I've got to get to Neuve Albuquerque immediately."

The expressionless voice said, "The next rocket leaves at sixteen hours."

'Sixteen hours! I've got to be at the spaceport by that time!"

The voice said dispassionately, "We are sorry."

The bottom fell out of everything. Ronny said, desperately, "Look, if I miss my ship in Neuve Albuquerque, what is the next spaceliner leaving from there for New Delos?"

"A moment, citizen." There was an agonized wait, and then the voice said, "There is a liner leaving for New Delos on the 14th of next month. It arrives in New Delos on the 31st, Basic Earth calendar."

The 31st! Tommy Paine could be halfway across the galaxy by that time.

A gentle voice next to him said, "Could I help, Ronny?"

He looked around at her. "Evidently, nobody can," he said disgustedly. "There's no way of getting to Neuve Albuquerque in time to get that cruiser to New Delos."

Tog Lee Chang Chu fished in her bag and came up with a wallet similar to the one in which Ronny carried his Section G badge. She held it up to the screen. "Bureau of Investigation, Section G," she said calmly. "It will be necessary that Agent Bronston and myself be in Neuve Albuquerque within the hour."

The metallic voice said, "Of course. Proceed to your right and through Corridor K to Exit Four. Your rocket will be there. Identify yourself to Lieutenant Economou who will be at the desk at Exit Four."

Tog turned to Ronny Bronston. "Shall we go?" she said demurely.

He cleared his throat, feeling foolish. "Thanks, Tog," he said.

"Not at all, Ronny. Why, this is my job."

Was there the faintest of sarcasm in her voice? It hadn't been more than a couple of hours ago that he had been hinting rather heavily to Sid Jakes that he needed no assistance.

She even knew the layout of the West Greater Washington shuttleport. Her small body swiveled through the hurrying passengers, her small feet a-twinkle, as she led him to and down Corridor K and then to the desk at Exit Four.

Ronny anticipated her here. He flashed his own badge at the chair-borne Space Forces lieutenant there.

"Lieutenant Economou?" he said. "Ronald Bronston, of the Bureau of Investigation, Section G. We've got to get to Neuve Albuquerque soonest."

The lieutenant, only mildly impressed, said, "We can have you in the air in ten minutes, citizen. Just a moment and I'll guide you myself."

* * * * *

In the rocket, Ronny had time to appraise her at greater length. She was a delicately pretty thing, although her expression was inclined to the over-serious. There was only a touch of the Mongolian fold at the corner of her eyes. On her it looked unusually good. Her complexion was that which only the blend of Chinese and Caucasian can give. Her figure, thanks to her European blood, was fuller than Eastern Asia usually boasts; tiny, but full.

Let's admit it, he decided. My assistant is the cutest trick this side of a Tri-Di movie queen, and we're going to be thrown in the closest of juxtaposition for an indefinite time. This comes under the head of work?

He said, "Look here, Tog, you were with Sid Jakes longer than I was. What's the full story?"

She folded her slim hands in her lap, looking like a schoolgirl about to recite. "Do you know anything about the socio-economic system on New Delos?"

"Well, no," he admitted.

She said severely, "I'd think that they would have given you more background before an assignment of this type."

Ronny said impatiently, "In the past three months I've been filled in on the economic systems, the religious beliefs, the political forms, of a thousand planets. I just happened to miss New Delos."

Her mouth expressed disapproval by rucking down on the sides, which was all very attractive but also irritating. She said, "There are two thousand, four hundred and thirty-six member planets in the UP, I'd think an agent of Section G would be up on the basic situation on each."

He had her there. He said snidely, "Hate to contradict you, Tog, but the number is two thousand, four hundred and thirty-four."

"Then," she nodded agreeably, "membership has changed since this morning when Menalaus and Aldebaran Three were admitted. Have two planets dropped out?"

"Look," he said, "let's stop bickering. What's the word on New Delos?"

"Did you ever read Frazer's 'Golden Bough'?" she said.

"No."

"You should. At any rate, New Delos is a theocracy. A priesthood elite rules it. A God-King, who is immortal, holds absolute authority. The strongest of superstition plus an efficient inquisition, keeps the people under control."

"Sounds terrible," Ronny growled.

"Why? Possibly the government is extremely efficient and under it the planet progressing at a rate in advance of UP averages."

He stared at her in surprise.

She said, "Would you rather be ruled by the personal, arbitrary whims of supremely wise men, or by laws formulated by a mob?"

It stopped him momentarily. In all his adult years, he couldn't remember ever meeting an intelligent, educated person who had been opposed to the democratic theory.

"Wait a minute, now," he said. "Who decides that they're supremely wise men who are doing this arbitrary ruling? Let any group come to power, by whatever means, and they'll soon tell you they're an elite. But let's get back to New Delos, from what you've said so far, the people are held in a condition of slavery."

"What's wrong with slavery?" Tog said mildly.

He all but glared at her. "Are you kidding?"

"I seldom jest," Tog said primly. "Under the proper conditions, slavery can be the most suitable system for a people."

"Under *what* conditions!"

"Have you forgotten your Earth history to the point where Egypt, Greece and Rome mean nothing to you? Man made some of his outstanding progress under slavery. And do you contend that man's lot is necessarily miserable given slavery? As far back as Aesop we know of slaves who have reached the heights in their society. Slaves sometimes could and did become the virtual rulers in ancient countries." She shrugged prettily. "The prejudices which you hold today, on Earth, do not necessarily apply to all time, nor to all places."

He said, impatiently, "Look, Tog, we can go into this further, later. Let's get back to New Delos. What happened?"

Tog said, "The very foundation of their theocracy is the belief on the part of the populace that the God-King is immortal. No man conspires against his Deity. Supervisor Jakes informed me that it is understood by UP Intelligence, that about once every twenty years the priesthood secretly puts in a new God-King. Plastic surgery would guarantee facial resemblance, and, of course, the rank and file citizen would probably never be allowed close enough to discover that their God-King seemed different every couple of decades. At any rate, it's been working for some time."

"And there's been no revolt against this religious aristocracy?"

She shook her head. "Evidently not. It takes a brave man to revolt against both his king and his God at the same time."

"But what happened now?" Ronny pursued.

"Evidently, right in the midst of a particularly important religious ceremony, with practically the whole planet watching on TV, the God-King was killed with a bomb. No doubt about it, definitely killed. There are going to be a lot of people on New Delos wondering how it can be that an immortal God-King can die."

"And Sid thinks it's Tommy Paine's work?"

She shifted dainty shoulders in a shrug. "It's the sort of thing he does. I suppose we'll learn when we get there."

* * * * *

Even on the fast Space Forces cruiser, the trip was going to take a week, and there was precious little Ronny Bronston could do until arrival. He spent most of his time reading up on New Delos and the several other planets in the UP organization which had fairly similar regimes. More than a few theocracies had come and gone during the history of man's development into the stars.

He also spent considerable time playing Battle Chess or talking with Tog and with the ship's officers.

These latter were a dedicated group, high in morale, enthusiastic about their work which evidently involved the combined duties of a Navy, a Coast Guard, and a Coast and Geodetic Survey system, if we use the ocean going services of an earlier age for analogy.

They all had the dream. The enthusiasm of men participating in a race's expansion to glory. There was the feeling, even stronger here in space than back on Earth, of man's destiny being fulfilled, that humanity had finally emerged from its infancy, that the fledgling had finally found its wings and got off the ground.

After one of his studying binges, Ronny Bronston had spent an hour or so once with the captain of the craft, while that officer stood an easy watch on the ship's bridge. There was little enough to do in space, practically nothing, but there was always an officer on watch.

They leaned back in the acceleration chairs before the ship's controls and Ronny listened to the other's space lore. Stories of far planets, as yet untouched. Stories of planets that had seemingly been suitable for colonization, but had proved disastrous for man, for this reason or that.

Ronny said, "And never in all this time have we run into a life form that has proved intelligent?"

Captain Woiski said, "No. Not that I know of. There was an animal on Shangri-La of about the mental level of the chimpanzee. So far as I know, that's the nearest to it."

"Shangri-La?" Ronny said. "That's a new one."

There was an affectionate gleam in the captain's eye. "Yes," he said. "If and when I retire, I think that'd be the planet of my choice, if I could get permission to leave Earth, of course."

Ronny scowled in attempted memory. "Now that you mention it, I think I did see it listed the other day among planets with a theocratic government."

The captain grunted protest. "If you're comparing it to this New Delos you're going to, you're wrong. There can be theocracy and theocracy, I suppose. Actually, I imagine Shangri-La has the most, well *gentle* government in the system."

Ronny was interested. His recent studies hadn't led him to much respect for a priesthood in political power. "What's the particular feature that's seemed to have gained your regard?"

"Moderation," Woiski chuckled. "They carry it almost to the point of immoderation. But not quite. Briefly, it works something like this. They have a limited number of monks —I suppose you'd call them-who spend their time at whatever moves them. At the arts, at scientific research, at religious contemplation-any religion will do-as students of anything and everything, and at the governing of Shangri-La. They make a point of enjoying the luxuries in moderation and aren't a severe drain on the rank and file citizens of the planet."

Ronny said, "I have a growing distrust of hierarchies. Who decides who is to become a monk and who remain a member of the rank and file?"

The captain said, "A series of the best tests they can devise to determine a person's intelligence and aptitudes. From earliest youth, the whole populace is checked and rechecked. At the age of thirty, when it is considered that a person has become adult and has finished his basic education, a limited number are offered monkhood. Not all want it."

Ronny thought about it. "Why not? What are the shortcomings?"

The captain shrugged. "Responsibility, I suppose."

"The monks aren't allowed sex, booze, that sort of thing, I imagine."

"Good heavens, why not? In moderation, of course."

"And they live on a higher scale?"

"No, no, not at all. Don't misunderstand. The planet is a prosperous one. Exceedingly prosperous. There is everything needed for comfortable existence for everyone. Shangri-La is one planet where the pursuit of happiness is pursuable by all." Captain Woiski chuckled again.

Ronny said, "It sounds good enough, although I'm leery of benevolent dictatorships. The trouble with them is that it's up to the dictators to decide what's benevolent. And almost always, nepotism rears its head, favoritism of one sort or another. How long will it be before one of your moderate monks decides he'll moderately tinker with the tests, or whatever, just to be sure his favorite nephew makes the grade? A high I.Q. is no guarantee of integrity."

The captain didn't disagree. "That's always possible, I suppose. One guard against it, in this case, is the matter of motive. The *privilege* of being a monk isn't as great as all that. Materially, you aren't particularly better off than any one else. You have more leisure, that's true, but actually most of them are so caught up in their studies or research that they put in more hours of endeavor than does the farmer or industrial worker on Shangri-La."

"Well," Ronny said, "let's just hope that Tommy Paine never hears of this place."

"Who?" the captain said.

Ronny Bronston reversed his engines. "Oh, nobody important. A guy I know of."

Captain Woiski scowled. "Seems to me I've heard the name."

At first Ronny leaned forward with quick interest. Perhaps the cruiser's skipper had a lead. But, no, he sank back into his chair. That name was strictly a Section G pseudonym. No one used it outside the department, and he'd already said too much by using the term at all.

Ronny said idly, "Probably two different people. I think I'll go on back and see how Tog is doing."

* * * * *

Tog was at her communicator when he entered the tiny ship's lounge. Ronny could see in the brilliant little screen of the compact device, the grinning face of Sid Jakes. Tog looked up at Ronny and smiled, then clicked the device off.

"What's new?" Ronny said.

She moved graceful shoulders. "I just called Supervisor Jakes. Evidently there's complete confusion on New Delos. Mobs are storming the temples. In the capital the priests tried to present a new God-King and he was laughed out of town."

Ronny snorted cynically. "Sounds good to me. The more I read about New Delos and its God-King and his priesthood, the more I think the best thing that ever happened to the planet was this showing them up."

Tog looked at him, the sides of her mouth tucking down as usual when she was going to contradict something he said. "It sounds bad to me," she said. "Tommy Paine's work is done. He'll be off to some other place and we won't get there in time to snare him."

Ronny considered that. It was probably true. "I wonder," he said slowly, "if it's possible for us to get a list of all ships that have blasted off since the assassination, all ships and their destination from New Delos."

The idea grew in him. "Look! It's possible that a dictatorial government such as theirs would immediately quarantine every spaceport on the planet."

Tog said, "There's only one spaceport on New Delos. The priesthood didn't encourage trade or even communication with the outside. Didn't want its people contaminated."

"Holy smokes!" Ronny blurted. "It's possible that Tommy Paine's on that planet and can't get off. Look, Tog, see if you can raise the Section G representative on New Delos and —"

Tog said demurely, "I already have taken that step, Ronny, knowing that you'd want me to. Agent Mouley Hassan has promised to get the name and destination of every passenger that leaves New Delos."

Ronny sat down at a table and dialed himself a mug of stout. "Drink?" he said to Tog. "Possibly we've got something to celebrate."

She shook her head disapprovingly. "I don't use depressants."

There was nothing more to be discussed about New Delos, they simply would have to wait until their arrival. Ronny switched subjects. "Ever hear of the planet Shangri-La?" he asked her. He took a sip of his brew.

"Of course," she said. "A rather small planet, Earth type within four degrees. Noted for its near perfect climate and its scenic beauty."

"Captain was talking about it," Ronny said. "Sounds like a regular paradise."

Tog made a negative sound.

"Well, what's wrong with Shangri-La?" Ronny said impatiently.

"Static," she said briefly.

He looked at her. "It sounds to me as though it's developed a near perfect socio-economic system. What do you mean, static?"

"No push, no drive," Tog said definitely. "Everyone-what is the old term? —everyone has it made. The place is stagnating. I wouldn't be surprised to see Tommy Paine show up there sooner or later."

Ronny said, "Look, since we've known each other, have I ever said anything you agree with?"

Tog raised her delicate eyebrows. "Why, Ronny. You know perfectly well we both agreed that the eggs for breakfast were quite inedible."

Ronny came to his feet again. Considering her size, she certainly was an irritating baggage. "I think I'll go to my room and see if I can get any inspirations on tracking down our quarry."

"Good night, Ronny," she said demurely.

* * * * *

They ran into a minor difficulty upon arrival at New Delos. The captain called both Ronny Bronston and Tog Lee Chang Chu to the bridge.

He nodded in the direction of the communications screen. A bald headed, robed character- obviously a priest-scowled at them.

Captain Woiski said, "The Sub-Bishop informs me that the provisional government has ruled that any spacecraft landing on New Delos cannot take off again without permission and that every individual who lands, even United Planets personnel, will need an exit visa before being allowed to depart."

Ronny said, "Then you can't land?"

The captain said reasonably, "My destination is Merlini. I've gone out of my way slightly to drop you off here. But I can't afford to take the chance of having my ship tied up for what might be an indefinite period. Evidently, there's considerably civil disorder down there."

From the screen the priest snapped, "That is an inaccurate manner of describing the situation."

"Sorry," the captain said dryly.

Ronny Bronston said desperately, "But, captain, Miss Tog and I simply have to land." He reached for his badge. "High priority, Bureau of Investigation."

The captain shrugged his hefty shoulders. "Sorry, I have no instructions that allow me to risk tying up my ship. Here's a possibility. Can you pilot a landing craft? I could spare you one, then you and your assistant would be the only ones involved. You could turn it over to whatever Space Forces base we have here."

Ronny said miserably, "No. I'm not a space pilot."

"I am," Tog said softly. "The idea sounds excellent."

"We shall expect you," the Sub-Bishop said. The screen went blank.

Tog Lee Chang Chu piloted a landing craft with the same verve that she seemed to be able to handle any other responsibility. As he sat in the seat next to her, Ronny Bronston took in her practiced flicking of the controls from the side of his eyes. He wondered vaguely at the efficiency of such Section G officials as Metaxa and Jakes that they would assign an unknown quality such as himself to a task as important as running down Tommy Paine, and then as an assistant provide him with an experienced operative such as Tog. The bureaucratic mind can be a dilly, he decided. Was the fact that she was a rather delicately constructed girl a factor? He felt the weight of the Model-H gun nestled under his left armpit. Perhaps in the clutch Section G preferred men as agents.

They swooped into a landing that brought them as close to the control tower as was practical. In a matter of moments there was a guard of twenty or more sloppily uniformed men about their small craft.

Tog made a move. "Welcoming committee," she said.

They climbed out the circular port, and flashed their United Planets Bureau of Investigation badges to the

They climbed out the circular port, and flashed their United Planets Bureau of Investigation badges to the youngish looking soldier who seemed in command. He was indecisive.

"United Planets?" he said. "All I know is I'm supposed to arrest anybody landing."

Ronny snapped, "We're to be taken immediately to United Planets headquarters."

"Well, I don't know about that. I don't take orders from foreigners."

One of his men was nervously fingering the trigger of his submachine gun.

Ronny's mouth went dry. He had the feeling of being high, high on a rock face, inadequately belayed from above.

Tog said smoothly, "But, major, I'm sure whoever issued your orders had no expectation of a special delegation from the United Planets coming to congratulate your new authorities on their success. Of course, it's unknown to arrest a delegation from United Planets."

"It is?" he frowned at her. "I mean, you are?"

"Yes," Tog said sweetly.

Ronny took the hint. "Where can we find a vehicle, major, to get us to the capital and to United Planets headquarters? Evidently we arrived before we were expected. There should have been a big welcoming committee here."

"Oh," the obviously recently promoted lad said hesitantly. "Well, I suppose we can make arrangements. This way please." He grinned at Tog as they walked toward the administration building. "Do all girls dress like you on Earth?"

"Well, no," she said demurely.

"That's too bad," he said gallantly.

"Why, major!" Tog said, keeping her eyes on the tarmac.

At the administration building there was little of order, but eventually they managed to arrange for their transportation. Luckily, they were supplied with a chauffeur driven helio-car.

Luckily, because without the chauffeur to help them run the gauntlet they would have been held up by parades, demonstrations and monstrous street meetings a dozen times before they ever reached their destination. Twice, Ronny stopped short of drawing his gun only by a fraction when half drunken demonstrators stopped them.

The driver, a wispy, sad looking type, shook his head. "There's no going back now," he told them over his shoulder. "No going back. Last week I was all with the rest, I never did believe David the One was really Immortal. But you was just used to the idea, see? It'd always been that way, with the priests running everything and we was used to it. Now I wish we was still that way. At least you knew how you stood, see? Now, what's going to happen?"

"That's an interesting question," Tog said politely.

Ronny said, "Possibly you'll have the chance to build a better world, now."

The driver shot a contemptuous look over his shoulder. "Better world? What do I want with a better world? I just don't want to be bothered. I've been getting my three squares a day, got a nice little flat for my family. How do I know it's not going to be a worse world?"

"That's always a possibility," Tog told him. "Do most people seem to feel the same?"

"Practically everybody I know does," he said glumly. "But the fat's in the fire now. The priests are trying to hold on but their government is falling apart all over the place."

"Well," Ronny said, "at least you can figure just about anything in the way of a new government will be better than one based on superstition and inquisition. It couldn't get worse."

"Things can always get worse," the other contradicted him sadly.

* * * * *

They left the cab before an impressively tall, many windowed building in city center. As they mounted the steps, Ronny frowned at her. "You seemed to be encouraging that man in his pessimism. So far as I can see, the best thing that ever happened to this planet was toppling that phony priesthood."

"Perhaps," she said agreeably. "However, the man's mind was an ossified one. A surprisingly large percentage of people have them, especially when it comes to institutions such as religion and government. We weren't going to be able to teach him anything, but it was possible to learn from him."

Ronny grunted his disgust. "What could we possibly learn from him?"

Tog said mildly, "We could learn what people of the street were thinking. It might give us some ideas about what direction the new government will take."

They approached the portals of the building and were halted by an armed Space Forces guard of half a dozen men. Their sergeant saluted, taking in their obvious other-planet clothing.

"Identifications, please," he said briskly.

They showed their badges and were passed on through. Ronny said to him, "Much trouble, sergeant?"

The other shrugged. "No. Just precautions, sir. We've been here only three or four weeks. Civil disturbance. We're used to it. Were over on Montezuma two basic months ago. Now there was *real* trouble. Had to shoot our way out."

Tog called, "Coming Ronny? I have this elevator waiting."

He followed her, scowling. An idea was trying to work its way through. Somehow he missed getting it.

Headquarters of the Department of Justice were on the eighth floor. A receptionist clerk led them through three or four doors to the single office which housed Section G.

A red eyed, exhausted agent looked up from the sole desk and snarled a question at them. Ronny didn't get it, but Tog said mildly, "Probationary Agent Ronald Bronston and Tog Lee Chang Chu. On special assignment." She flicked open her badge so that the other could see it.

His manner changed. "Sorry," he said, getting up to shake hands. "I'm Mouley Hassan, in charge of Section G on New Delos. We've just had a crisis here, as you can imagine. The worst of it's now over." He added sourly, "I hope. All my assistants have already taken off for Avalon." He was a short statured, dark complected man, his features betraying his Semitic background.

Ronny shook hands with him and said, "Sorry to bother you at a time like this."

They found chairs and Mouley Hassan flicked a key on his order box and said to them, "How about a drink? They make a wonderful sparkling wine on this planet. Trust any theocracy to have top potables."

Ronny accepted the offer, Tog refused it politely. She sat demurely, her hands in her lap.

Mouley Hassan ran a weary hand through already mussed hair. "What's this special assignment you're on?"

Ronny said, "Commissioner Metaxa has sent me looking for Tommy Paine."

"Tommy Paine!" the other blurted. "At a time like this, when I haven't had three nights' sleep in the last three basic weeks, you come around looking for Tommy Paine?"

Ronny was taken aback. "Sid Jakes seemed to think this might be one of Paine's jobs."

Tog said mildly, "What better place to look for Tommy Paine, than in a situation like this, Agent Hassan?" Her eyebrows went up. "Or don't you think the quest for Paine is an important one?"

The other subsided somewhat. "I suppose you're right," he said. "I'm deathly tired. Do whatever you want. But don't expect much from me."

Tog said, just a trifle tartly, Ronny thought, "We'll have to call on you, as usual, Agent Hassan. There's probably no single job in Section G more important than the pursuit of Tommy Paine."

"All right, all right," Mouley Hassan admitted. "I'll co-operate. How long have you been away from Earth?" he said to Ronny.

"About one basic week."

"Oh," he grunted. "This is your first stop, eh? Well, I don't envy you your job." He brought a cool bottle from a delivery drawer in the desk along with two glasses. "Here's the wine."

Ronny leaned forward to accept the glass. "This situation here," he said, "do you think it can be laid to Paine?"

Mouley Hassan shrugged wearily. "I don't know."

Ronny sipped the drink, looking at the tired agent over the glass rim. "From what we understand, check has been kept on all persons leaving the planet since the bombing."

"Check is right. There's only one ship that took off and it carried nobody except my assistants. If you ask me, I still needed them, but some brass hat back on Earth decided they were more necessary over on Avalon." He was disgusted.

Ronny put the glass down. "You mean only one ship's left this planet since the God-King was killed?"

"That's right. It was like pulling teeth to get the visas."

"How many men aboard?"

Mouley Hassan looked at him speculatively. "Four-man crew and six Section G operatives."

Tog said brightly, "Why, that means, then, that either Tommy Paine is still on this planet, or he's one of the passengers or crew members of that ship." She added, "That is, of course, unless he had a private craft, hidden away somewhere."

Ronny slumped back into his chair as some of the ramifications came home to him. "If it was Tommy Paine at all," he said.

Mouley Hassan nodded. "That's always a point." He finished his glass and looked pleadingly at Tog. "Look, I have work. If I can finish some of it, I might have time for some sleep. Couldn't we postpone the search for Tommy Paine."

Tog said nothing to him.

Ronny came to his feet. "We'll get along. A couple of ideas occur to me. I'll check with you later."

"Fine," the agent said. He shook hands with them again. He said, somehow more to Tog than to Ronny, "I know how important your job is. It's just that I've been pushed to the point where I can't operate efficiently."

She smiled her understanding, gave him her small, delicate hand.

In the elevator, Ronny said to her, "Why should this sort of thing particularly affect Section G?"

Tog said, "It's times like this that planets drop out of the UP. Or, possibly, get into the hands of some jingoistic military group and start off halfcocked to provoke a war with some other planet, or to missionarize or propagandize it." She thought about it a moment. "A new revolution, in government or religion, seems almost invariably to want to spread the light. An absolute compulsion to bring to others the new truths that they've found." She added, her voice holding a trace of mockery, "Usually the new truths are rather hoary ones, and there are few interested in hearing them."

* * * * *

They spent their first day in getting accommodations in a centrally located hotel, in making arrangements, through the Department of Justice, for the local means of exchange-it turned out to be coinage, based on gold-and getting the feel of their surroundings.

Evidently Delos, the capital city of the planet New Delos, was but slowly emerging from the chaos that had taken over on the assassination. A provisional government, composed of representatives of half a dozen different organizations which had sprung up like mushrooms following the collapse of the regime, had assumed power. Elections had been promised and were to be brought off when arrangements could be made.

Meanwhile, the actual government was still largely in the hands of the lower echelons of the priesthood. A nervous priesthood it was, seemingly desirous of getting out from under while the going was good, afraid of being held responsible for former excesses.

Ronny Bronston, high hopes still in his head, looked up the Sub-Bishop who had given them landing orders while they were still aboard the Space Forces cruiser. Tog was off making arrangements for various details involved in their being in Delos in its time of crisis.

A dozen times, on his way over to keep his appointment with the official, Ronny had to step into doorways, or in other wise make himself inconspicuous. Gangs of demonstrators roamed the street, some of them drunken, looking for trouble, and scornful of police or the military. Twice, when it looked as though he might be roughed up, Ronny drew his gun and held it in open sight, ready for use, but not threateningly. The demonstrators made off.

His throat was dry by the time he reached his destination. The life of a Section G agent, on interplanetary assignment, had its drawbacks.

The Sub-Bishop had formerly been in charge of Interplanetary Communications which involved commerce as well as intercourse with United Planets. It must have been an ultra-responsible position only a month ago. Now his offices were all but deserted.

He looked at Ronny's badge, only vaguely interested. "Section G of the Bureau of Investigation," he said. "I don't believe I am aware of your responsibilities. However," he nodded with sour courtesy, "please be seated. You must forgive my lack of ability to offer refreshment. Isn't there an old tradition about rats deserting a sinking ship? I am afraid my former assistants had rodentlike instincts."

Ronny said, "Section G deals with Interplanetary Security, sir —"

"I am addressed as Holiness," the other said.

Ronny looked at him. "Sorry," he said. "I am a citizen of the United Planets, not any one planet, even Earth. UP citizens have complete religious freedom. In my case I am unaffiliated with any church."

The Sub-Bishop let it pass. He said sourly, "I am afraid that even here on New Delos, I am seldom honoured by my title any more. Go on, you say you deal with Interplanetary Security."

"That's correct. In cases like this we're interested in checking to see if there is any possibility that citizens of planets other than New Delos are involved in your internal affairs."

The other's eyes were suddenly slits. He said, heavily, "You suspect that David the One was assassinated by an alien?"

Ronny had to tread carefully here. "I make no such suggestion. I am merely here to check on the possibility. If such was the case, my duty would be to arrest the man, or men."

"If we got hold of him, you'd have small chance of asserting your authority," the priest growled. "What did you want to know?"

"I understand that no interplanetary craft have left New Delos since the assassination."

"None except a United Planets ship which was carefully inspected."

Ronny said tightly, "But what facilities do you have to check on secret spaceports, possibly located in some remote desert or mountain area?"

The New Delian laughed sourly. "There is no other planet in all the United Planets with our degree of security. We even imported the most recent developments in artificial satellites equipped with the most delicate of detection devices. I assure you, it is utterly impossible for a spacecraft to land or take off from New Delos without our knowledge."

Ronny Bronston's eyes lit with excitement. "These security measures of yours. To what extent do you keep under observation all aliens on the planet?"

The priest's chuckle had a nasty quality. "You are quite ignorant of our institutions, evidently. Every person on New Delos, in every way of life, was under constant survey from the cradle to the grave. Aliens were highly discouraged. When they appeared on New Delos at all, they were restricted in their movements to this, our capital city."

Ronny let air whistle from his lungs. "Then," he said triumphantly, "if any alien had anything to do with this, he is still on the planet. Can you get me a list of all aliens?"

The other laughed again, still sourly. "But there are none. None except you employees of United Planets. I'm afraid you're on a wild-goose chase."

Ronny stared at him blankly. "But commercial representatives, cultural exchange —"

The priest said flatly, "No. None at all. All commerce was handled through UP. We encouraged no cultural exchanges. We wished to keep our people uncorrupted. United Planets alone had the right to land on our one spaceport."

The Section G agent came to his feet. This was much simpler than he could ever have hoped for. He thanked the other, but avoided the necessity of shaking hands, and left.

* * * * *

He found a helio-cab and dialed it to the UP building, finding strange the necessity of slipping coins into the vehicle's slots until the correct amount for his destination had been deposited. Coinage was no longer in use on Earth.

At the UP building he retraced his steps of the day before to the single office of Section G.

To his surprise, not only Mouley Hassan was there, but Tog as well. Hassan had evidently had at least a few hours of sleep. He was in better shape.

They exchanged the usual amenities and took their chairs again.

Hassan said, "We were just gossiping. It's been years since I've been in Greater Washington. Lee Chang tells me that Sid Jakes is now a Supervisor. I worked with him for a while, when I first joined Section G. How about a glass of wine?"

Ronny said, "Look. If Tommy Paine was connected with this, and it's almost positive he was, we've got him."

The others looked at him.

"You've evidently been busy," Tog said mildly.

He turned to her. "He's trapped, Tog! He can't get off the planet."

Mouley Hassan rubbed a hand through his hair. "It'd be hard, all right. They've got the people under rein here such as you've never seen before. Or they did until this blew up."

Ronny sketched the situation to Tog, winding up with, "The only thing that makes sense is that it's a Tommy Paine job. The local citizens would never have been able to get their hands on such a bomb, or been able to have made the arrangements for its delivery. They're under too much surveillance."

Tog said thoughtfully, "but how did he escape all this surveillance?"

"Don't you understand? He's working here, in this building, as an employee of UP. There is no other alternative."

They stared at him.

"I think perhaps you're right," Tog said finally.

Ronny turned to Mouley Hassan. "Can you get a list of all UP employees?"

"Of course." He flicked his order box, barked a command into it.

Ronny said, "It's going to be a matter of eliminating the impossible. For instance, what is the earliest known case of Tommy Paine's activity?"

Tog thought back. "So far as we know definitely, about twenty-two years ago."

"Fine," Ronny said, increasingly excited. "That will eliminate all persons less than, say, forty years of age. We can assume he was at least twenty when he began."

Hassan said, "Can we eliminate all women employees?"

Ronny said, "I'd think so. The few times he's been seen, all reports are of a man. And that case on the planet Mother where he put himself over as a Holy Man. He could hardly have been a woman in disguise in a Stone Age culture such as that."

Hassan said, "And this Tommy Paine has been flitting around this part of the galaxy for years, so anyone who has been here steadily for a period of even a couple of years or so, can't be suspect."

Mouley Hassan thrust his hand into a delivery drawer and brought forth a handful of punched cards, possibly fifty in all.

"Surely there's more people than that working in this building," Ronny protested.

Mouley Hassan said, "No. I've eliminated already everyone who is a citizen of New Delos. Obviously, Tommy Paine is an alien. We have only forty-eight Earthlings and other United Planets citizens working here."

He carried the cards to a small collator and worked for a moment on its controls, as Tog and Ronny watched him with mounting tension. "Let's see," he muttered. "We eliminate all women, all those less than forty, all who haven't done a great deal of travel, those who have been here for several years."

The end of it was that they eliminated everyone employed in the UP building.

The cards were stacked back on Mouley Hassan's desk again, and the three of them sat around and looked glumly at them.

Ronny said, "He's tinkered with the files. He counterfeited fake papers for himself, or something. Possibly he's pulled his own card and it isn't in this stack you have."

Mouley Hassan said, "We'll double-check all those possibilities, but you're wrong. Possibly a few hundred years ago, but not today. Forgery and counterfeiting are things of the past. And, believe me, the Bureau of Investigation and especially Section G, may look on the slipshod side, but they aren't. We're not going to find anything wrong with those cards. Tommy Paine simply is not working for UP on New Delos."

"Then," Ronny said, "there's only one alternative. He's on this UP ship going to, what was the name of its destination?"

"Avalon," Mouley Hassan said, his face thoughtful.

Tog said, "Do you have any ideas on the men aboard?"

Mouley Hassan said, "There were four crew men, and six of our agents."

Tog said, "Unless one of them has faked papers, the six agents are eliminated. That leaves the crew members. Do you know anything about them?"

Hassan shook his head.

Ronny said, "Let's communicate with Avalon. Tell our representatives there to be sure that none of the occupants of that ship leaves Avalon until we get there."

Mouley Hassan said, "Good idea." He turned to his screen and said into it, "Section G, Bureau of Investigation, on the Planet Avalon."

In moment the screen lit up. An elderly agent, as Section G agents seemed to go, looked up at them.

Mouley Hassan held his silver badge so the other could see it and on the Avalon agent's nod said, "I'm Hassan from New Delos. We've just had a crisis here and there seems to be a chance that it's a Tommy Paine job. Agent Bronston here is on an assignment tracking him down. I'll turn it over to Bronston."

The Avalon agent nodded again, and looked at Ronny.

Ronny said urgently, "We haven't the time to give you details, but every indication is that Paine is on a UP spacecraft with Avalon as its destination. There are only ten men aboard, and six of them are Section G operatives."

The other pursed his lips. "I see. You think you have the old fox cornered, eh?"

"Possibly," Ronny said. "There are various ifs. Miss Tog and I can double check here. Then as soon as we can clear exit visas, we'll make immediate way for Avalon."

The Avalon Section G agent said, "I haven't the authority to control the movements of other agents, they have as high rank as I have," he added, expressionlessly, "and probably higher than yours."

Ronny said, "But the four-man crew?"

The other said, "These men are coming to Avalon to work on a job that will take at least six months. We'll make a routine check, and I'll try and make sure the whole ten will still be on Avalon when and if you arrive."

They had to be satisfied with that. They checked all ways from the middle, nor did it take long. There was no doubt. If this was a Tommy Paine job, and it almost surely was, then there was only one way in which he could have escaped from the planet and that was by the single spacecraft that had left, destination Avalon. He was not on the planet, that was definite Ronny felt. A stranger on New Delos was as conspicuous as a walrus in a goldfish bowl. There simply were no such.

They spent most of their time checking and rechecking United Planets personnel, but there was no question there either.

Mouley Hassan and others of UP personnel helped cut the red tape involved in getting exit visas from New Delos. It wasn't as complicated as it might have been a week or two before. No one seemed to be so confident of his authority in the new provisional government that he dared veto a United Planets request.

Mouley Hassan was able to arrange for a small space yacht, slower than a military craft, but capable of getting them to Avalon in a few days time. A one-man crew was sufficient, Ronny, and especially Tog, could spell him on the watches.

Time aboard was spent largely in studying up on Avalon, going over and over again anything known about the elusive Tommy Paine, and playing Battle Chess and bickering with Tog Lee Chang Chu.

If it hadn't been for this ability to argue against just about anything Ronny managed to say, he could have been attracted to her to the detriment of the job. She was a good traveler, few people are; she was an ultra-efficient assistant; she was a joy to look at; and she never intruded. But, Great Guns, the woman could bicker.

The two of them were studying in the ship's luxurious lounge when Ronny looked up and said, "Do you have any idea why those six agents were sent to Avalon?"

"No," she said.

He indicated the booklet he was reading. "From what I can see here, it sounds like one of the most advanced planets in the UP. They've made some of the most useful advances in industrial techniques of the past century."

"Oh, I don't know," Tog mused. "I haven't much regard for Industrial Feudalism myself. It starts off with a bang, but tends to go sterile."

"Industrial feudalism," he said indignantly. "What do you mean? The government is a constitutional monarchy with the king merely a powerless symbol. The standard of living is high. Elections are honest and democratic. They've got a three-party system...."

"Which is largely phony," Tog interrupted. "You've got to do some reading between the lines, especially when the books you're reading are turned out by the industrial feudalistic publishing companies in Avalon."

"What's this industrial feudalism, you keep talking about? Avalon has a system of free enterprise."

"A gobbledygook term," Tog said, irritatingly. "Industrial feudalism is a socio-economic system that develops when industrial wealth is concentrated into the hands of a comparatively few families. It finally gets to the point of a closed circle all but impossible to break into. These industrial feudalistic families become so powerful that only in rare instances can anyone lift himself into their society. They dominate every field, including the so-called labor unions, which amount to one of the biggest businesses of all. With their unlimited resources they even own every means of dispensing information."

"You mean," Ronny argued, "that on Avalon you can't start up a newspaper of your own and say whatever you wish?"

"Certainly you can, theoretically. If you have the resources. Unfortunately, such enterprises become increasingly expensive to start. Or you could start a radio, TV or Tri-Di station-if you had the resources. However, even if you overcame all your handicaps and your newspaper or broadcasting station became a success, the industrial feudalistic families in control of Avalon's publishing and broadcasting fields have the endless resources to buy you out, or squeeze you out, by one nasty means or another."

Ronny snorted. "Well, the people must be satisfied or they'd vote some fundamental changes."

Tog nodded. "They're satisfied, and no wonder. Since childhood every means of forming their opinions have been in the hands of industrial feudalistic families-including the schools."

"You mean the schools are private?"

"No, they don't have to be. The government is completely dominated by the fifty or so families which for all practical purposes own Avalon. That includes the schools. Some of the higher institutions of learning are private, but they, too, are largely dependent upon grants from the families."

* * * * *

Ronny was irritated by her know-all air. He tapped the book he'd been reading with a finger. "They don't control the government. Avalon's got a three-party system. Any time the people don't like the government, they can vote in an alternative."

"That's an optical illusion. There are three parties, but each is dominated by the fifty families, and election laws are such that for all practical purposes it's impossible to start another party. Theoretically it's possible, actually it isn't. The voters can vary back and forth between the three political parties but it doesn't make any difference which one they elect. They all stand for the same thing —a continuation of the status quo."

"Then you claim it isn't democracy at all?"

Tog sighed. "That's a much abused word. Actually, pure democracy is seldom seen. They pretty well had it in primitive society where government was based on the family. You voted for one of your relatives in your clan to represent you in the tribal councils. Every one in the tribe was equal so far as apportionments of the necessities of life were concerned. No one, even the tribal chiefs, ate better than anyone else, no one had a better home."

Ronny said, snappishly, "And if man had remained at that level, we'd never have gotten anywhere."

"That's right," she said. "For progress, man needed a leisure class. Somebody with the time to study, to experiment, to work things out."

He said, "We're getting away from the point. You said in spite of appearances they don't have democracy on Avalon."

"They have a pretense of it. But only free men can practice democracy. So long as your food, clothing and shelter are controlled by someone else, you aren't free. Wait until I think of an example." She put her right forefinger to her chin, thoughtfully.

Holy smokes, she was a cute trick. If only she wasn't so confounded irritating.

Tog said, "Do you remember the State of California in Earth history?"

"I think so. On the west coast of North America."

"That's right. Well, back in the Twentieth Century, Christian calendar, they had an economic depression. During it a crackpot organization called Thirty Dollars Every Thursday managed to get itself on the ballot. Times were bad enough but had this particular bunch got into power it would have become chaotic. At first no thinking person took them seriously, however a majority of people in California at that time had little to lose and in the final week or so of the election campaign the polls showed that Thirty Dollars Every Thursday was going to win. So, a few days before voting many of the larger industries and businesses in the State ran full page ads in the newspapers. They said substantially the same thing. *If Thirty Dollars Every Thursday wins this election, our concern will close its doors. Do not bother to come back to work Monday.* "

Ronny was scowling at her. "What's your point?"

She shrugged delicate shoulders. "The crackpots were defeated, of course, which was actually good for California. But my point is that the voters of California were not actually free since their livelihoods were controlled by others. This is an extreme case, of course, but the fact always applies."

A thought suddenly hit Ronny Bronston. "Look," he said. "Tommy Paine. Do you think he's merely escaping from New Delos, or is it possible that Avalon is his next destination? Is he going to try and overthrow the government there?"

She was shaking her head, but frowning. "I don't think so. Things are quite stable on Avalon."

"Stable?" he scowled at her. "From what you've been saying, they're pretty bad."

She continued to shake her head. "Don't misunderstand, Ronny. On an assignment like this, it's easy to get the impression that all the United Planets are in a state of socio-political confusion, but it isn't so. A small minority of planets are ripe for the sort of trouble Tommy Paine stirs up. Most are working away, developing, making progress, slowly evolving. Avalon is one of these. The way things are there, Tommy Paine couldn't make a dent on changing things, even if he wanted to, and there's no particular reason to believe he does."

Ronny growled. "From what I can learn of the guy he's anxious to stir up trouble wherever he goes."

"I don't know. If there's any pattern at all in his activities, it seems to be that he picks spots where things are ripe to boil over on their own. He acts as a catalyst. In a place like Avalon he wouldn't get to first base. Possibly fifty years from now, things will have developed on Avalon to the point where there is dissatisfaction. By that time," she said dryly, "we'll assume Tommy Paine will no longer be a problem to the Commissariat of Interplanetary Affairs for one reason or the other."

Ronny took up his book again. He growled, "I can't figure out his motivation. If I could just put my finger on that."

For once she agreed with him. "I've got an idea, Ronny, that once you have that, you'll have Tommy Paine."

* * * * *

They drew blank on Avalon.

Or, at least, it was drawn for them before they ever arrived.

The Section G agent permanently assigned to that planet had already checked and double checked the possibilities. None of the four-man crew of the UP spacecraft had been on New Delos at the time of the assassination of the God-King. They, and their craft, had been light-years away on another job.

Ronny Bronston couldn't believe it. He simply couldn't believe it.

The older agent, his name was Jheru Bulchand, was definite. He went over it with Ronny and Tog in a bar adjoining UP headquarters. He had dossiers on each of the ten men, detailed dossiers. On the face of it, none of them could be Paine.

"But one of them has to be," Ronny pleaded. He explained their method of eliminating the forty-eight employees of UP on New Delos.

Bulchand shrugged. "You've got holes in that method of elimination. You're assuming Tommy Paine is an individual, and you have no reason to. My own theory is that it's an organization."

Ronny said unhappily, "Then you're of the opinion that there is a Tommy Paine?"

The older agent was puffing comfortably on an old style briar pipe. He nodded definitely. "I believe Tommy Paine exists as an organization. Possibly once, originally, it was a single person, but now it's a group. How large, I wouldn't know. Probably not too large or by this time somebody would have betrayed it, or somebody would have cracked and we would have caught them. Catch one and you've got the whole organization what with our modern means of interrogation."

Tog said, "I've heard the opinion before."

Jheru Bulchand pointed at Ronny with his pipe stem. "If its an organization, then none of that eliminating you did is valid. Your assassin could have been one of the women. He could have been one of the men you eliminated as too young-someone recently admitted to the Tommy Paine organization."

Ronny checked the last of his theories. "Why did Section G send six of its agents here?"

"Nothing to do with Tommy Paine," Bulchand said. "It's a different sort of crisis."

"Just for my own satisfaction, what kind of crisis?"

Bulchand sketched it quickly. "There are two Earth type planets in this solar system. Avalon was the first to be colonized and developed rapidly. After a couple of centuries, Avalonians went over and settled on Catalina. They eventually set up a government of their own. Now Avalon has a surplus of industrial products. Her economic system is such that she produces more than she can sell back to her own people. There's a glut."

Tog said demurely, "So, of course, they want to dump it in Catalina."

Bulchand nodded. "In fact, they're willing to give it away. They've offered to build railroads, turn over ships and aircraft, donate whole factories to Catalina's slowly developing economy."

Ronny said, "Well, how does that call for Section G agents?"

"Catalina has evoked Article Two of the UP Charter. No member planet of UP is to interfere with the internal political, socio-economic or religious affairs of another member planet. Avalon claims the Charter doesn't apply since Catalina belongs to the same solar system and since she's a former colony. We're trying to smooth the whole thing over, before Avalon dreams up some excuse for military action."

Ronny stared at him. "I get the feeling every other sentence is being left out of your explanation. It just doesn't make sense. In the first place, why is Avalon as anxious as all that to give away what sounds like a fantastic amount of goods?"

"I told you, they have a glut. They've overproduced and, as a result, they've got a king-size depression on their hands, or will have unless they find markets."

"Well, why not trade with some of the planets that want her products?"

Tog said as though reasoning with a youngster, "Planets outside her own solar system are too far away for it to be practical even if she had commodities they didn't. She needs a nearby planet more backward than herself, a planet like Catalina."

"Well, that brings us to the more fantastic question. Why in the world doesn't Catalina accept? It sounds to me like pure philanthropy on the part of Avalon."

Bulchand was wagging his pipe stem in a negative gesture. "Bronston, governments are never motivated by idealistic reasons. Individuals might be, and even small groups, but governments never. Governments, including that of Avalon, exist for the benefit of the class or classes that control them. The only things that motivate them are the interests of that class."

"Well, this sounds like an exception," Ronny said argumentatively. "How can Catalina lose if the Avalonians grant them railroads, factories and all the rest of it?"

Tog said, "Don't you see, Ronny? It gives Avalon a foothold in the Catalina economy. When the locomotives wear out on the railroad, new engines, new parts, must be purchased. They won't be available on Catalina because there will be no railroad industry because none will have ever grown up. Catalina manufacturers couldn't compete with that initial free gift. They'll be dependent on Avalon for future equipment. In the factories, when machines wear out, they will be replaceable only with the products of Avalon's industry."

Bulchand said, "There's an analogy in the early history of the United States. When its fledgling steel industry began, they set up a high tariff to protect it against British competition. The British were amazed and indignant, pointing out that they could sell American steel products at one third the local prices, if only allowed to do so. The United States said no thanks, it didn't want to be tied, industrially, to Great Britain's apron strings. And in a couple of decades American steel production passed England's. In a couple of more decades American steel production was many times that of England's and she was taking British markets away from her all over the globe."

"At any rate," Ronny said, "it's not a Tommy Paine matter."

Just for luck, though, Ronny and Tog double checked all over again on Bulchand's efforts. They interviewed all six of the Section G agents. Each of them carried a silver badge that gleamed only for the individual who possessed it. All of which eliminated the possibility that Paine had assumed the identity of a Section G operative. So that was out.

They checked the four crew members, but there was no doubt there, either. The craft had been far away at the time of the assassination on New Delos.

On the third day, Ronny Bronston, disgusted, knocked on the door of Tog's hotel room. The door screen lit up and Tog, looking out at him said, "Oh, come on in, Ronny, I was just talking to Earth."

He entered.

Tog had set up her Section G communicator on a desk top and Sid Jakes' grinning face was in the tiny, brilliant screen. Ronny approached close enough for the other to take him in.

Jakes said happily, "Hi, Ronny, no luck, eh?"

Ronny shook his head, trying not to let his face portray his feelings of defeat. This after all was a probationary assignment, and the supervisor had the power to send Ronny Bronston back to the drudgery of his office job at Population Statistics.

"Still working on it. I suppose it's a matter of returning to New Delos and grinding away at the forty-eight employees of the UP there."

Sid Jakes pursed his lips. "I don't know. Possibly this whole thing was a false alarm. At any rate, there seems to be a hotter case on the fire. If our local agents have it straight, Paine is about to pull one of his coups on Kropotkin. This is a top-top-secret, of course, one of the few times we've ever detected him before the act."

Ronny was suddenly alert, his fatigue of disgust of but a moment ago, completely forgotten. "Where?" he said.

"Kropotkin," Jakes said. "One of the most backward planets in UP and seemingly a setup for Paine's sort of trouble making. The authorities, if you can use the term applied to Kropotkin, are already complaining, threatening to invoke Article One of the Charter, or to resign from UP." Jake looked at Tog again. "Do you know Kropotkin, Lee Chang?"

She shook her head. "I've heard of it, rather vaguely. Named after some old anarchist, I believe."

"That's the place. One of the few anarchist societies in UP. You don't hear much from them." He turned to Ronny again. "I think that's your bet. Hop to it, boy. We're going to catch this Tommy Paine guy, or organization, or whatever, soon or United Planets is going to know it. We can't keep the lid on indefinitely. If word gets around of his activities, then we'll lose member planets like Christmas trees shedding needles after New Year's." He grinned widely. "That's sounds like a neat trick, eh?"

* * * * *

91

Ronny Bronston had got to the point where he avoided controversial subjects with Tog even when provoked and she had a sneaky little way of provoking arguments. They had only one really knock down and drag-out verbal battle on the way to Kropotkin.

It had started innocently enough after dinner on the space liner on which they had taken passage for the first part of the trip. To kill time they were playing Battle Chess with its larger board and added contingents of pawns and castles.

Ronny said idly, "You know, in spite of the fact that I'm a third generation United Planets citizen and employee, I'm just beginning to realize how far out some of our member planets are. I had no idea before."

She frowned in concentration, before moving. She was advancing her men in echelon attack, taking losses in exchange for territory and trying to pen him up in such small space that he couldn't maneuver.

She said, "How do you mean?"

Ronny lifted and dropped a shoulder. "Well, New Delos and its theocracy, for instance, and Shangri-La and Mother and some of the other planets with extremes in government of socio-economic system. I hadn't the vaguest idea about such places."

She made a deprecating sound. "You should see Amazonia, or, for that matter, the Orwellian State."

"*Amazonia* ," he said, "does that mean what it sounds like it does?"

She made her move and settled back in satisfaction. Her pawns were in such position that his bishops were both unusable. He'd tried to play a phalanx game in the early stages of her attack, but she'd broken through, rolling up his left flank after sacrificing a castle and a knight.

"Certainly does," she said. "A fairly recently colonized planet. A few thousand feminists no men at all-moved onto it a few centuries ago. And it's still an out and out matriarchy."

Ronny cleared his throat delicately. "Without men ...ah, how did they continue several centuries?"

Tog suppressed her amusement. "Artificial insemination, at first, so I understand. They brought their, ah, supply with them. But then there were boys among the first generation on the new planet and even the Amazonians weren't up to cold bloodedly butchering their children. So they merely enslaved them. Nice girls."

Ronny stared at her. "You mean all men are automatically slaves on this planet?"

"That's right."

Ronny made an improperly thought out move, trying to bring up a castle to reinforce his collapsing flank. He said, "UP allows *anybody* to join evidently," and there was disgust in his voice.

"Why not?" she said mildly.

"Well, there should be *some* standards."

Tog moved quickly, dominating with a knight several squares he couldn't afford to lose. She looked up at him, her dark eyes sparking. "The point of UP is to include all the planets. That way at least conflict can be avoided and some exchange of science, industrial techniques and cultural gains take place. And you must remember that while in power practically no socio-economic system will admit to the fact that it could possibly change for the better. But actually there is nothing less stable. Socio-economic systems are almost always in a condition of flux. Planets such as Amazonia might for a time seem so brutal in their methods as to exclude their right to civilized intercourse with the rest. However, one of these days there'll be a change-or one of these centuries. They all change, sooner or later." She added softly, "Even Han."

"Han?" Ronny said.

Her voice was quiet. "Where I was born, Ronny. Colonized from China in the very early days. In fact, I spent my childhood in a commune." She said musingly, "The party bureaucrats thought their system an impregnable, unchangeable one. Your move."

Ronny was fascinated. "And what happened?" He was in full retreat now, and with nowhere to go, his pieces pinned up for the slaughter. He moved a pawn to try and open up his queen.

"Why don't you concede?" she said. "Tommy Paine happened."

"Paine!"

"Uh-huh. It's a long story. I'll tell you about it some time." She pressed closer with her own queen.

He stared disgustedly at the board. "Well, that's what I mean," he muttered. "I had no idea there were so many varieties of crackpot politico-economic systems among the UP membership."

"They're not necessarily crackpot," she protested mildly. "Just at different stages of development."

"Not crackpot!" he said. "Here we are heading for a planet named Kropotkin which evidently practices anarchy."

"Your move," she said. "What's wrong with anarchism?"

He glowered at her, in outraged disgust. Was it absolutely impossible for him to say anything without her disagreement?

Tog said mildly, "The anarchistic ethic is one of the highest man has ever developed." She added, after a moment of pretty consideration. "Unfortunately, admittedly, it hasn't been practical to put to practice. It will be interesting to see how they have done on Kropotkin."

"Anarchist ethic, yes," Ronny snapped. "I'm no student of the movement but the way I understand it, there isn't any."

Tog smiled sweetly. "The belief upon which they base their teachings is that no man is capable of judging another."

Ronny cast his eyes ceilingward. "O.K., I give up!"

She began rapidly resetting the pieces. "Another game?" she said brightly.

"Hey! I didn't mean the game! I was just about to counterattack."

"Ha!" she said.

* * * * *

The Section G agent on Kropotkin was named Hideka Yamamoto, but he was on a field tour and wouldn't be back for several days. However, there wasn't especially any great hurry so far as Ronny Bronston and Tog Lee Chang Chu knew. They got themselves organized in the rather rustic equivalent of a hotel, which was located fairly near UP headquarters, and took up the usual problems of arranging for local exchange, meals, means of transportation and such necessities.

It was a greater problem than usual. In fact, hadn't it been for the presence of the UP organization, which had already gone through all this the hard way, some of the difficulties would have been all but insurmountable.

For instance, there was no local exchange. There was no medium of exchange at all. Evidently simple barter was the rule.

In the hotel-if it could be called a hotel-lobby, Ronny Bronston looked at Tog. "Anarchism!" he said. "Oh, great. The highest ethic of all. And what's the means of transportation on this wonderful planet? The horse. And how are we going to get a couple of horses with no means of exchange?"

She tinkled laughter.

"All right," he said. "You're the Man Friday. You find out the details and handle them. I'm going out to take a look around the town-if you can call this a town."

"It's the capital of Kropotkin," Tog said placatingly, though with a mocking background in her tone. "Name of Bakunin. And very pleasant, too, from what little I've seen. Not a bit of smog, industrial fumes, street dirt, street noises —"

"How could there be?" he injected disgustedly. "There isn't any industry, there aren't any cars, and for all practical purposes, no streets. The houses are a quarter of a mile or so apart."

She laughed at him again. "City boy," she said. "Go on out there and enjoy nature a little. It'll do you good. Anybody who has cooped himself up in that one big city, Earth, all his life ought to enjoy seeing what the great outdoors looks like."

He looked at her and grinned. She was cute as a pixie, and there were no two ways about that. He wondered for a moment what kind of a wife she'd make. And then shuddered inwardly. Life would be one big contradiction of anything he'd managed to get out of his trap.

He strolled idly along what was little more than a country path and it came to him that there were probably few worlds in the whole UP where he'd have been prone to do this within the first few hours he'd been on the planet. He would have been afraid, elsewhere, of anything from footpads to police, from unknown vehicles to unknown traffic laws. There was something bewildering about being an Earthling and being set down suddenly in New Delos or on Avalon.

Here, somehow, he already had a feeling of peace.

Evidently, although Bakunin was supposedly a city, its populace tilled their fields and provided themselves with their own food. He could see no signs of stores or warehouses. And the UP building, which was no great edifice itself, was the only thing in town which looked even remotely like a governmental building.

Bakunin was neat. Clean as a pin, as the expression went. Ronny was vaguely reminded of a historical Tri-Di romance he'd once seen. It had been laid in ancient times in a community of the Amish in old Pennsylvania.

He approached one of the wooden houses. The things would have been priceless on Earth as an antique to be erected as a museum in some crowded park. For that matter it would have been priceless for the wood it contained. Evidently, the planet Kropotkin still had considerable virgin forest.

An old-timer smoking a pipe, sat on the cottage's front step. He nodded politely.

Ronny stopped. He might as well try to get a little of the feel of the place. He said courteously, "A pleasant evening."

The old-timer nodded. "As evenings should be after a fruitful day's toil. Sit down, comrade. You must be from the United Planets. Have you ever seen Earth?"

Ronny accepted the invitation and felt a soothing calm descend upon him almost immediately. An almost disturbingly pleasant calm. He said, "I was born on Earth."

"Ai?" the old man said. "Tell me. The books say that Kropotkin is an Earth type planet within what they call a few degrees. But is it? Is Kropotkin truly like the mother planet?"

Ronny looked about him. He'd seen some of this world as the shuttle rocket had brought them down from the passing liner. The forests, the lakes, the rivers, and the great sections untouched by man's hands. Now he saw the areas between homes, the neat fields, the signs of human toil-the toil of hands, not machines.

"No," he said, shaking his head. "I'm afraid not. This is how Earth must once have been. But no longer."

The other nodded. "Our total population is but a few million," he said. Then, "I would like to see the mother planet, but I suppose I never shall."

Ronny said diplomatically, "I have seen little of Kropotkin thus far but I am not so sure but that I might not be happy to stay here, rather than ever return to Earth."

The old man knocked the ashes from his pipe by striking it against the heel of a work-gnarled hand. He looked about him thoughtfully and said, "Yes, perhaps you're right. I am an old man and life has been good. I suppose I should be glad that I'll unlikely live to see Kropotkin change."

"Change? You plan changes?"

* * * * *

The old man looked at him and there seemed to be a very faint bitterness, politely suppressed. "I wouldn't say *we* planned them, comrade. Certainly not we of the older generation. But the trend toward change is already to be seen by anyone who wishes to look, and our institutions won't long be able to stand. But, of course, if you're from United Planets you would know more of this than I."

"I'm sorry. I don't know what you're talking about."

"You are new indeed on Kropotkin," the old man said. "Just a moment." He went into his house and emerged with a small power pack. He indicated it to Ronny Bronston. "This is our destruction," he said.

The Section G agent shook his head, bewildered.

The old-timer sat down again. "My son," he said, "runs the farm now. Six months ago, he traded one of our colts for a small pump, powered by one of these. It was little use on my part to argue against the step. The pump eliminates considerable work at the well and in irrigation."

Ronny still didn't understand.

"The power pack is dead now," the old man said, "and my son needs a new one."

"They're extremely cheap," Ronny said. "An industrialized planet turns them out in multi-million amounts at practically no cost."

"We have little with which to trade. A few handicrafts, at most."

Ronny said, "But, good heavens, man, build yourselves a plant to manufacture power packs. With a population this small, a factory employing no more than half a dozen men could turn out all you need."

The old man was shaking his head. He held up the battery. "This comes from the planet Archimedes," he said, "one of the most highly industrialized in the UP, so I understand. On Archimedes do you know how many persons it takes to manufacture this power pack?"

"A handful to operate the whole factory, Archimedes is fully automated."

The old man was still moving his head negatively. "No. It takes the total working population of the planet. How many different metals do you think are contained in it, in all? I can immediately see what must be lead and copper."

Ronny said uncomfortably, "Probably at least a dozen, some in microscopic amounts."

"That's right. So we need a highly developed metallurgical industry before we can even begin. Then a developed transportation industry to take metals to the factory. We need power to run the factory, hydro-electric, solar, or possibly atomic power. We need a tool-making industry to equip the factory, the transport industry and the power industry. And while the men are employed in these, we need farmers to produce food for them, educators to teach them the sciences and techniques involved, and an entertainment industry to amuse them in their hours of rest. As their lives become more complicated with all this, we need a developed medical industry to keep them in health."

The old man hesitated for a moment, then said, "And, above all, we need a highly complicated government to keep all this accumulation of wealth in check and balance. No. You see, my friend, it takes *social labor* to produce products such as this, and thus far we have avoided that on Kropotkin. In fact, it was for such avoidance that my ancestors originally came to this planet."

Ronny said, scowling, "This gets ridiculous. You show me this basically simple power pack and say it will ruin your socio-economic system. On the face of it, it's ridiculous."

The old man sighed and looked out over the village unseeingly. "It's not just that single item, of course. The other day one of my neighbors turned up with a light bulb with built-in power for a year's time. It is the envy of the unthinking persons of the neighborhood most of whom would give a great deal for such a source of light. A nephew of mine has somehow even acquired a powered bicycle, I think you call them, from somewhere or other. One by one, item by item, these products of advanced technology turn up-from whence, we don't seem to be able to find out."

Under his breath, Ronny muttered, "*Paine!* "

"I beg your pardon," the old man said.

"Nothing," the Section G agent said. He leaned forward and, a worried frown working its way over his face, began to question the other more closely.

Afterwards, Ronny Bronston strode slowly toward the UP headquarters. There was only a small contingent of United Planets personnel on this little populated member planet but, as always, there seemed to be an office for Section G.

Ronny stood outside it for a moment. There were voices from within, but he didn't knock.

In fact, he cast his eyes up and down the short corridor. At the far end was a desk with a girl in the Interplanetary Cultural Exchange Department working away in concentration. She wasn't looking in his direction.

Ronny Bronston put his ear to the door. The building was primitive enough, rustic enough in its construction, to permit his hearing.

Tog Lee Chang Chu was saying seriously, "Oh, it was chaotic all right, but no, I don't really believe it could have been a Tommy Paine case. Actually I'd suggest to you that you run over to Catalina. When I was on Avalon I heard rumors that Tommy Paine's finger seemed to be stirring around in the mess there. Yes, I'd recommend that you take off for Catalina immediately. If Paine is anywhere in this vicinity at all, it would be Catalina."

For a moment, Ronny Bronston froze. Then in automatic reflex his hand went inside his jacket to rest over the butt of the Model H automatic there.

No, that wasn't the answer. His hand dropped away from the gun.

He listened, further.

Another voice was saying, "We thought we were on the trail for a while on Hector, but it turned out it wasn't Paine. Just a group of local agitators fed up with the communist regime there. There's going to be a blood bath on Hector, before they're through, but it doesn't seem to be Paine's work this time."

Tog's voice was musing. "Well, you never know, it sounds like the sort of muck he likes to play in."

The strange voice said argumentatively, "Well, Hector *needs* a few fundamental changes."

"It could be," Tog said, "but that's their internal affairs, of course. Our job in Section G is to prevent troubles between the differing socio-economic and religious features of member planets. Whatever we think of some of the things Paine does, our task is to get him."

Ronny Bronston pushed the door open and went through. Tog Lee Chang Chu was sitting at a desk, nonchalant and petitely beautiful as usual, comfortably seated in easy-chairs were two young men by their attire probably citizens of United Planets and possibly even Earthlings.

"Hello, Ronny," Tog said softly. "Meet Frederic Lippman and Pedro Nazaré, both Section G operatives. This is my colleague, Ronald Bronston, gentlemen. Fredric and Pedro were just leaving, Ronny."

The two agents got up to shake hands.

Ronny said, "You can't be in that much of a hurry. What's your assignment, boys?"

Lippman, an earnest type, and by his appearance not more than twenty-five or so years of age, began to answer, but Nazaré said hurriedly, "Actually, it's a confidential assignment. We're working directly out of the Octagon."

Lippman said, frowning, "It's not that confidential, Tog. Bronston's an agent, too. What's your assignment, Ronny?"

Ronny said very slowly, "I'm beginning to suspect that it's the same as yours and various pieces are beginning to fall into place."

Lippman was taken aback. "You mean you're looking for Tommy Paine?" His eyes went to his associate. "How could that be, Tog? I didn't know more than one of us were on this job. Why, that means if Bronston here finds him first, I won't get my permanent appointment."

Ronny looked at Tog Lee Chang Chu who was sitting demurely, hands in lap, and a resigned expression on her face. He said, "Nor if you find him first, will I. Look here, Tog, how many men does Sid Jakes have out on this assignment?"

"I wouldn't know," she said mildly.

He snapped, "A few dozen or so? Or possibly a few hundred?"

"It seems unlikely there could be that many," she said mildly. She looked at the other two agents. "I think you two had better run along. Take my suggestion I made earlier."

"Wait a minute," Ronny snapped. "You mean that they go to Catalina? That's ridiculous."

Tog Lee Chang Chu looked at Pedro Nazaré and he turned and started for the door followed by Fredric Lippman who was still scowling his puzzlement.

"Wait a minute!" Ronny snapped. "I tell you it's ridiculous. And why follow her suggestions? She's just my assistant."

Pedro Nazaré said, "Come on, Fred, let's get going, we'll have to pack." But Lippman wasn't having any.

"His assistant?" he said to Tog Lee Chang Chu.

Tog Lee Chang Chu's face changed expression in sudden decision. She opened her bag and brought forth a Section G identification wallet and flicked it open. The badge was gold. "I suggest you hurry," she said to the two agents.

They left, and Tog turned back to Ronny, her eyebrows raised questioningly.

Ronny sank down into one of the chairs recently occupied by the other two agents and tried to unravel thoughts. He said finally, "I suppose my question should be, why do Ross Metaxa and Sid Jakes send an agent of supervisor rank to act as assistant to a probationary agent? But that's not what I'm asking yet. First, Lippman just called his buddy Tog. How come?"

Tog took her seat again, rueful resignation on her face. "You should be figuring it out on your own by this time, Ronny."

He looked at her belligerently. "I'm too stupid, eh?" The anger was growing within him.

"Tog," she said. "It's a nickname, or possibly you might call it a title. Tog. T-O-G. The Other Guy. My name is Lee Chang Chu, and I'm of supervisor grade presently working at developing new Section G operatives. Considering the continuing rapid growth of UP, and the continuing crises that come up in UP activities, developing new operatives is one of the department's most pressing jobs. Each new agent, on his first assignment, is always paired with an experienced old-timer."

"I see," he said flatly. "Your principal job being to needle the fledging, eh?"

She lowered her eyes. "I wouldn't exactly word it that way," she said. She was obviously unrepentant.

He said, "You must get a lot of laughs out of it. If I say, it seems to me democracy is a good thing, you give me an argument about the superiority of rule by an elite. If I say anarchism is ridiculous, you dredge up an opinion that it's man's highest ethic. You must laugh yourself to sleep at nights. You and Metaxa and Jakes and every other agent in Section G. Everybody is in on the Tog gag but the sucker."

"Sometimes there are amusing elements to the work," Lee Chang conceded, demurely.

"Just one more thing I'd like to ask," Ronny rapped. "This first assignment, agents are given. Is it always to look for Tommy Paine?"

She looked up at him, said nothing, but her eyes were questioning.

"Don't worry," he snapped. "I've already found out who Paine is."

"Ah?" She was suddenly interested. "Then I'm glad I ordered that other probationary agent to leave. Evidently, he hasn't. Obviously, I didn't want the two of you comparing notes."

"No, that would never do," he said bitterly. "Well, this is the end of the assignment so far as you and I are concerned. I'm heading back for Earth."

"Of course," she said.

* * * * *

He had time on the way to think it all over, and over and over again, and a great deal of it simply didn't make sense. He had enough information to be disillusioned, sick at heart. To have crumbled an idealistic edifice that had taken a lifetime to build. A lifetime? At least three. His father and his grandfather before him had had the dream. He'd been weaned on the idealistic purposes of the United Planets and man's fated growth into the stars.

He was a third-generation dreamer of participating in the glory. His grandfather had been a citizen of Earth and gave up a commercial position to take a job that amounted to little more than a janitor in an obscure department of Interplanetary Financial Clearing. He wanted to get into the big job, into space, but never made it. Ronny's father managed to work up to the point where he was a supervisor in Interplanetary Medical Exchange, in the tabulating department. He, too, had wanted into space, and never made it. Ronny had loved them both. In a way fulfilling his own dreams had been a debt he owed them, because at the same time he was fulfilling theirs.

And now this. All that had been gold, was suddenly gilted lead. The dream had become contemptuous nightmare.

Finally back in Greater Washington, he went immediately from the shuttleport to the Octagon. His Bureau of Investigation badge was enough to see him through the guide-guards and all the way through to the office of Irene Kasansky.

She looked up at him quickly. "Hi," she said. "Ronny Bronston, isn't it?"

"That's right. I want to see Commissioner Metaxa."

She scowled. "I can't work you in now. How about Sid Jakes?"

He said, "Jakes is in charge of the Tommy Paine routine, isn't he?"

She shot a sharper look up at him. "That's right," she said warily.

"All right," Ronny said. "I'll see Jakes."

Her deft right hand slipped open a drawer in her desk. "You'd better leave your gun here," she said. "I've known probationary agents to get excited, in my time."

He looked at her.

And she looked back, her gaze level.

Ronny Bronston shrugged, slipped the Model H from under his armpit and tossed it into the drawer.

Irene Kasansky went back to her work. "You know the way," she said.

This time Ronny Bronston pushed open the door to Sid Jakes' office without knocking. The Section G supervisor was poring over reports on his desk. He looked up and grinned his Sid Jakes' grin.

"Ronny!" he said. "Welcome back. You know, you're one of the quickest men ever to return from a Tommy Paine assignment. I was talking to Lee Chang only a day or so ago. She said you were on your way."

Ronny grunted, his anger growing within him. He lowered himself into one of the room's heavy chairs, and glared at the other.

Sid Jakes chuckled and leaned back in his chair. "Before we go any further, just to check, who is Tommy Paine?"

Ronny snapped, "You are."

The supervisor's eyebrows went up.

Ronny said, "You and Ross Metaxa and Lee Chang Chu-and all the rest of Section G. Section G is Tommy Paine."

"Good man!" Sid Jakes chortled. He flicked a switch on his order box. "Irene," he said, "how about clearing me through to the commissioner? I want to take Ronny in for his finals."

Irene snapped back something and Sid Jakes switched off and turned to Ronny happily. "Let's go," he said. "Ross is free for a time."

Ronny Bronston said nothing. He followed the other. The rage within him was still mounting.

In the months that had elapsed since Ronny Bronston had seen Ross Metaxa the latter had changed not at all. His clothing was still sloppy, his eyes bleary with lack of sleep or abundance of alcohol-or both. His expression was still sour and skeptical.

He looked up at their entry and scowled, and made no effort to rise and shake hands. He said to Ronny sourly, "O.K., sound off and get it over with. I haven't too much time this afternoon."

Ronny Bronston was just beginning to feel tentacles of cold doubt, but he suppressed them. The boiling anger was uppermost. He said flatly, "All my life I've been a dedicated United Planets man. All my life I've considered its efforts the most praiseworthy and greatest endeavor man has ever attempted."

"Of course, old chap," Jakes told him cheerfully. "We know all that, or you wouldn't ever have been chosen as an agent for Section G."

Ronny looked at him in disgust. "I've resigned that position, Jakes."

Jakes grinned back at him. "To the contrary, you're now in the process of receiving permanent appointment."

Ronny snorted his disgust and turned back to Metaxa. "Section G is a secret department of the Bureau of Investigation devoted to subverting Article One of the United Planets Charter."

Metaxa nodded.

"You don't deny it?"

Metaxa shook his head.

"Article One," Ronny snapped, "is the basic foundation of the Charter which every member of UP and particularly every citizen of United Planets, such as ourselves, has sworn to uphold. But the very reason for the existence of this Section G is to interfere with the internal affairs of member planets, to subvert their governments, their economic systems, their religions, their ideals, their very way of life."

Metaxa yawned and reached into a desk drawer for his bottle. "That's right," he said. "Anybody like a drink?"

Ronny ignored him. "I'm surprised I didn't catch on even sooner," he said. "On New Delos Mouley Hassan, the local agent, knew the God-King was going to be assassinated. He brought in extra agents and even a detail of Space Forces guards for the emergency. He probably engineered the assassination himself."

"Nope," Jakes said. "We seldom go *that* far. Local rebels did the actual work, but, admittedly, we knew what they were planning. In fact, I've got a sneaking suspicion that Mouley Hassan provided them with the bomb. That lad's a bit too dedicated."

"But *why* ," Ronny blurted. "That's deliberately interfering with internal affairs. If the word got out, every planet in UP would resign."

"Probably no planet in the system that needed a change so badly," Metaxa growled. "If they were ever going to swing into real progress, that hierarchy of priests had to go." He snorted. "An immortal God-King, yet."

Ronny pressed on. "That was bad enough, but how about this planet Mother, where the colonists had attempted to return to nature and live in the manner man did in earliest times."

"Most backward planet in the UP," Metaxa said sourly. "They just had to be roused."

"And Kropotkin!" Ronny blurted. "Don't you understand, those people were *happy* there. Their lives were simple, uncomplicated, and they had achieved a happiness that —"

Metaxa came to his feet. He scowled at Ronny Bronston and growled, "Unfortunately, the human race can't take the time out for happiness. Come along, I want to show you something."

He swung around the corner of his desk and made his way toward a ceiling-high bookcase. Ronny stared after him, taken off guard, but Sid Jakes was grinning his amusement.

Ross Metaxa pushed a concealed button and the bookcase slid away to one side to reveal an elevator beyond.

"Come along," Metaxa repeated over his shoulder. He entered the elevator, followed by Jakes.

There was nothing else to do. Ronny Bronston followed them, his face still flushed with the angered argument.

The elevator dropped, how far, Ronny had no idea. It stopped and they emerged into a plain, sparsely furnished vault. Against one wall was a boxlike affair that reminded Ronny of nothing so much as a deep-freeze.

For all practical purposes, that's what it was. Ross Metaxa led him over and they stared down into its glass-covered interior.

Ronny's eyes bugged. The box contained the partly charred body of an animal approximately the size of a rabbit. No, not an animal. It had obviously once been clothed, and its limbs were obviously those of a tool using life form.

Metaxa and Jakes were staring down at it solemnly, for once no inane grin on the supervisor's face. And that of Ross Metaxa was more weary than ever.

Ronny said finally, "What is it?" But he knew.

"You tell us," Metaxa growled sourly.

"It's an intelligent life form," Ronny blurted. "Why has it been kept secret?"

"Let's go on back upstairs," Metaxa sighed.

Back in his office he said, "Now I go into my speech. Shut up for a while." He poured himself a drink, not offering one to the other two. "Ronny," he said, "man isn't alone in the galaxy. There's other intelligent life. Dangerously intelligent."

In spite of himself Ronny reacted in amusement. "That little creature down there? The size of a small monkey?" As soon as he said it, he realized the ridiculousness of his statement.

Metaxa grunted. "Obviously, size means nothing. That little fellow down there was picked up by one of our Space Forces scouts over a century ago. How long he'd been drifting through space, we don't know. Possibly only months, but possibly hundreds of centuries. But however long he's proof that man is not alone in the galaxy. And we have no way of knowing when the expanding human race will come up against this other intelligence-and whoever it was fighting."

"But," Ronny protested, "you're assuming they're aggressive. Perhaps coming in contact with these aliens will be the best thing that ever happened to man. Possibly that little fellow down there is the most benevolent creature ever evolved."

Metaxa looked at him strangely. "Let's hope so," he said. "However, when found he was in what must have been a one-man scout. He was dead and his craft was blasted and torn-obviously from some sort of weapons' fire. His scout was obviously a military craft, highly equipped with what could only be weapons, most of them so damaged our engineers haven't been able to figure them out. To the extent they have been able to reconstruct them, they're scared silly. No, there's no two ways about it, our little rabbit sized intelligence down in the vault was killed in an interplanetary conflict. And sooner or later, Ronny, man in his explosion into the stars is going to run into either or both of the opponents in that conflict."

Ronny Bronston slumped back into his chair, his brain running out a dozen leads at once.

Metaxa and Jakes remained quiet, looking at him speculatively.

Ronny said slowly, "Then the purpose of Section G is to push the member planets of UP along the fastest path of progress, to get them ready for the eventual, inevitable meeting."

"Not just Section G," Metaxa growled, "but all of the United Planets organization, although most of the rank and file don't even know our basic purpose. Section G? We do the dirty work, and are proud to do it, by every method we can devise."

Ronny leaned forward. "But look," he said. "Why not simply inform all member planets of this common danger? They'd all unite in the effort to meet the common potential foe. Anything standing in the way would be brushed aside."

Metaxa shook his head wearily. "Would they? Is a common danger enough for man to change his institutions, particularly those pertaining to property, power and religion? History doesn't show it. Delve back into early times and you'll recall, for an example, that in man's early discovery of nuclear weapons he almost destroyed himself. Three or four different socio-economic systems co-existed at that time and all would have preferred destruction rather than changes in their social forms."

Jakes said, in an unwonted quiet tone, "No, until someone comes up with a better answer it looks as though Section G is going to have to continue the job of advancing man's institutions, in spite of himself."

The commissioner made it clearer. "It's not as though we deal with all our member planets. It isn't necessary. But you see, Ronny, the best colonists are usually made up of the, well, crackpot element. Those who are satisfied, stay at home. America, for instance, was settled by the adventurers, the malcontents, the non-conformists, the religious cultists, and even fugitives and criminals of Europe. So it is in the stars. A group of colonists go out with their dreams, their schemes, their far-out ideas. In a few centuries they've populated their new planet, and often do very well indeed. But often not and a nudge, a push, from Section G can start them up another rung or so of the ladder of social evolution. Most of them don't want the push. Few cultures, if any, realize they are mortal; like Hitler's Reich, they expect to last at least a thousand years. They resist any change-even change for the better."

* * * * *

Ronny's defenses were crumbling, but he threw one last punch. "How do you know the changes you make are for the better?"

Metaxa shrugged heavy shoulders. "It's sometimes difficult to decide, but we aim for changes that will mean an increased scientific progress, a more advanced industrial technology, more and better education, the opening of opportunity for every member of the culture to exert himself to the full of his abilities. The last is particularly important. Too many cultures, even those that think of themselves as particularly advanced, suppress the individual by one means or another."

Ronny was still mentally reeling with the magnitude of it all. "But how can you account for the fact that these alien intelligences haven't already come in contact with us?"

Metaxa shrugged again. "The Solar System, our sun, is way out in a sparsely populated spiral arm of our galaxy. Undoubtedly, these others are further in toward the center. We have no way of knowing how far away they are, or how many sun systems they dominate, or even how many other empires of intelligent life forms there are. All we know is that there are other intelligences in the galaxy, that they are near enough like us to live on the same type planets. The more opportunity man has to develop before the initial contact takes place, the stronger bargaining position, or military position, as the case may be, he'll be in."

Sid Jakes summed up the Tommy Paine business for Ronny's sake. "We need capable agents badly, but we need dedicated and efficient ones. We can't afford anything less. So when we come upon potential Section G operatives we send them out with a trusted Tog to get a picture of these United Planets of ours. It's the quickest method of indoctrination we've hit upon; the agent literally teaches himself by observation and participation. Usually, it takes four or five stops, on this planet and that, before the probationary agent begins sympathizing with the efforts of this elusive Tommy Paine. Especially since every Section G agent he runs into, including the Tog, of course, fills him full of stories of Tommy Paine's activities.

"You were one of the quickest to stumble on the true nature of our Section G. After calling at only three planets you saw that we ourselves are Tommy Paine."

"But ... but what's the end?" Ronny said plaintively. "You say our job is advancing man, even in spite of himself when it comes to that. We start at the bottom of the evolutionary ladder in a condition of savagery, clan communism in government, simple animism in religion, and slowly we progress through barbarism to civilization, through paganism to the higher ethical codes, through chattel slavery and then feudalism and beyond. What is the final end, the Ultima Thule?"

Metaxa was shaking his head again. He poured himself another drink, offered the bottle this time to the others. "We don't know," he said wearily, "perhaps there is none. Perhaps there is always another rung on this evolutionary ladder." He punched at his order box and said, "Irene, have them do up a silver badge for Ronny."

Ronny Bronston took a deep breath and reached for the brown bottle. "Well," he said. "I suppose I'm ready to ask for my first assignment." He thought for a moment. "By the way, if there's any way to swing it, I wouldn't mind working with Supervisor Lee Chang Chu."